LEAST SAID

SOONEST MENDED

BY

AGNES GIBERNE

AUTHOR OF

"KATHLEEN," "MISS CON," "READY, AYE READY!" ETC.

"He that refraineth his lips is wise."—PROV. x. 19.

"I had opened the shawl as I ran, and now I waved it wildly about."—*Page* 20.

CONTENTS.

—+—

"LEAST SAID, SOONEST MENDED."

CHAPTER I.

THE AFTERNOON EXPRESS.

THAT'S what my mother was fond of saying to me. "Least said, soonest mended, Kitty," says she, when people gossiped, or when folks got angry. And, dear me, there's a lot of hot words spoken, and a lot of gossip going on, and no mistake! Anyway, there was in those days when I was a girl. Talk! talk! the neighbours rattling like a set of parrots about anything and nothing. I'll not say either that the men were much better than the women, though there's no doubt they ought to be, seeing man was made superior.

"Least said, soonest mended, Kitty!" says my mother to me many a time, when she thought my tongue had been wagging too fast. Mother was a rare one for silence. Looking back now, I'm sure there's not many like her. She'd go for hours, and be quite content, never saying a word. I don't think she ever did speak just for the sake of speaking, and without a needs-be.

A

She wasn't dull either. Some silent people are dull; but not mother. For, you see, she didn't keep silent because she never had anything to say; and there was something about her very look that kept people alive.

I think I see her now—middle-aged, and going on for plumpness, with smooth brown hair, and a smooth forehead, and such a pair of quick eyes. Mother's eyes did a lot of speaking, when her lips were silent. Nothing ever escaped those eyes. She didn't always talk about what she saw, and she didn't forget it.

Mother was always neat, as if she had just come out of a band-box. She used to wear a brown stuff gown commonly, after her rough work of a morning was done, and a white apron. Every hour of the day, and every day of the week, had its own work. She never got into a muddle like the neighbours, who were for ever cleaning up, and for ever in a mess: and as for doing her washing "just any day," like them, she would have scorned the thought. I believe things would have been the same with her, if she had had a dozen children, instead of only one girl. But, after all, there's no knowing. It's a wonderful drag on a woman, to have a lot of children, and not enough money or room for the bringing of them up.

Well, I wasn't of mother's way of thinking about talk, for I did like to hear my own voice. Most girls do, I suppose; and it's only natural. But still I might have spared myself many a bother in life, if I had not been so ready with my tongue.

For, after all, the main part of the good and evil that we do in our lives is done with the tongue. Is not that what the Bible means, when it says that the man who can bridle his tongue is a perfect man? I suppose that is the hardest part of what we have to do. Mother must have come near to being a perfect woman, for the control she had over her tongue was something wonderful.

Father liked well enough to talk on occasion, but he was never a mischief-maker, and his tongue was not given to wagging ill-naturedly. Father was one of the kindest of men. I never saw him really out of temper in his life; and that's more than many children can say of their fathers. He was a thoughtful man, and he read a deal; and when he could get a sensible listener, he liked to talk about what he had read.

I am afraid I wasn't much of a listener, for I loved best to talk myself. Mother was always trying to check me; not harshly, but in the way of giving advice. " Waste of breath, Kitty, my dear," she'd say. " Keep your breath to cool your porridge." " Mind you, it's 'least said, soonest mended,' in the long run." " What's said can never be unsaid." And often she'd add—" We've got to give an account, by-and-by, of every idle word we speak. Every single idle word! "

But I don't think I paid heed to what she said. Young folks don't? Everybody has to learn out of his own experience, mostly; for experience can't be passed on from one to another like a sixpence. Perhaps mother pushed things a little too far. She saw the evil of careless talk, and she got to have almost a dread of any talk at all. After all, the power of talking is a gift, and it ought to be rightly used, not left to rust. We have influence over others by means of our talk, and we have to see that the influence isn't cast away, nor made to pull in the wrong direction.

I have spoken of neighbours, though there were no neighbours quite close to us. The nearest row of cottages was three minutes off, round the corner of the road that led from the station to the village. Beyond them came shops and a few other houses. Claxton was a small place, very scattered, and the railway-station was small too. My father was the station-master. A good many trains passed, but not many stopped.

Father had a cottage almost close to the line, and our garden was very gay. Flowers did so well with us—I don't know why, unless it was the soil, and his tending.

I was not an over-indulged child, like many only-children. My father and mother would not let me have my own way wrongly, and I was always made to obey. That's something to be thankful for. (Half the misery of many grown-up people comes from their never having learnt to submit in childhood.)

But though not indulged, I do think I was

rather spoilt; that's to say, I was made too much of, and I got to think myself too important, nobody being to blame particularly.

I suppose there's no denying that I was a pretty girl. I had dark eyes, and short curly brown hair, and a colour that came and went at a word. Then mother had trained me to be as particular as a lady about my dress and hair and hands. That does make a difference, to be sure. Nobody can look nice, if she don't keep her hair in order; and the prettiest girl in the world isn't pretty with a smudge on her cheek.

Father used to call me "his little wild rose," because of my colour and my shy manner; and Rupert used to talk of the way in which I dropped my eyes under their lashes.

Rupert Bowman was our ticket-collector. When I was seventeen, which is the time I am chiefly thinking about, he was over nineteen, not tall, but broad and strong, and a perfect slave to me. He had an honest plain face of his own, and a blunt way of speaking, commonly, which I think came from bashfulness. There wasn't a thing I could not make Rupert do, if I chose. He lived near with his widowed mother, and a sister; and he was in and out among us all day. Father liked Rupert ever so!

But about the spoiling,—I suppose it was a difficult thing to keep clear of. I had been a sickly child, often at home from school; and for years father and mother were in a fright every

winter lest they should lose me. At seventeen I
was much stronger, and had pretty well outgrown
the weakness ; but still I did not look strong, and
they could not get over the habit of always watching and thinking about me.

It was not my way to be cross-grained and dis-
contented like most spoilt girls. I can remember
being pretty nearly always happy. Good spirits
are a gift worth having, and I had very good spirits.
I liked seeing people, and I liked to know that they
counted me pretty and clever. I liked still more
to feel that I could make myself loved. People do
like that, women more especially, perhaps ; and
I don't say that the feeling is in itself wrong.
Only there is something wrong when a girl gets to
be always thinking about herself, and doing everything for the sake of being admired or loved. She
may be ever so pleasant, but none the less there's
something wrong. One ought to have a better
reason for doing.

So I think that on the whole I had more of love
and admiration in those days than is wholesome
for anybody. The harm did not show itself out-
wardly, perhaps, but it worked inwardly. Nobody
except mother ever crossed me ; and she never did
it in a sharp or vexing way.

My father's name was James Phrynne. He was
an old and trusted servant of the Company ; and he
had been station-master in Claxton for several years.
Mother's name was Jane, and mine was Kate, or
Kitty.

I can remember so well one Saturday afternoon
in June, that year when I was seventeen years old.

I had been for a walk on the common, which
was not fifteen minutes distant from the station.
Mother often sent me there "for a blow," if she
thought me looking pale. We did get lovely breezes
up on the common, that seemed to come straight
from the sea, though the sea was miles away. Sometimes I used to fancy I could taste salt on my lips,
when the wind blew hard.

I had been all the way across to the other side
and back, gathering a great bunch of the wild roses
which grew on the hedge surrounding part of the
common. Mother was so fond of wild roses.

When I got near home, Rupert came up. He
had been to his home for tea, and was on his way
back to the station, so he joined me. It was
natural he should : he and I were so much together.
I had always been fond of Rupert, and he was
always good to me. You see, I had no brothers
or sisters of my own, and Rupert had only one
sickly sister called Mabel,—much too fine a name
for such a poor fretful thing !

Not many people cared for Mabel Bowman ;
and though Rupert was in a way fond of her, he
thought much more of me. I think I liked to
know this. It was nice to feel that he would do
anything in the world for my sake. And yet I
should have liked Rupert to be different in many
ways from what he was. I used to wish him
handsome and clever, instead of plain and awk-

ward and dull. Everybody said he was such a good fellow, and that was true; but I was silly, and cared more for looks.

Still I did not at all mind having him for my humble slave, and being able to order him about.

Well, he came up to me that day, and said something about my bunch of roses.

" They are like you, Kitty," he says.

" I don't see it," said I.

" No, of course you don't; you can't see yourself," Rupert answered humbly, though in a sort of tone as if he was sure. "Look!" and he touched a pink blossom with his big hand.

I snatched it away, for I thought he would crush the delicate thing; and I always did tease Rupert for his clumsiness whenever I had a chance. He didn't seem to mind, commonly.

"Kitty, you needn't be afraid," he said in a hurt voice. " You don't think I'd be rough with anything *you* care for ? "

" I don't know. How can I tell ? " I asked. " You needn't handle my roses, any way. Don't you know you always smash whatever you take hold of."

" Not if it's yours, Kitty," says he.

" Oh, that don't make any difference," says I. "It's having such great huge fingers."

"I'd make them small if I could, but I can't," said he dolefully.

" You can't help it, of course ; but you can help spoiling my nosegay," I said.

Then I saw he really was put out at what I said, and I peeped up at him under my eyelashes in a way he called shy. It wasn't shy really. I knew I could come round Rupert in a moment with that peep.

"There, never mind," I said; "you needn't care. Nobody is ever cross with me, and you know I don't mean anything."

"There never was anybody like you, Kitty," says he, ready to forgive in a moment.

Then he walked by my side, quite silent for a minute, maybe more. I didn't know what had come over him.

"Kitty," says he at last.

"Yes," says I.

"Kitty," says he, and stuck fast again, for all the world as if he'd got into a slough of despond.

"Well," said I.

"Kitty," says he a third time, and looked as red and sheepish as anything.

"Yes," said I, for there was nothing else to be said.

"Kit—ty," says he a fourth time, very slow, as if he didn't know how to get it out.

And then all of a sudden I began to have a notion what was coming, and I didn't want it to come.

"Oh, look there!" I cried out.

"Where?" says he, and he stared all around.

"There; those clouds," I said. "Oh, look! Aren't they funny? There's one just exactly like a big whale, and a cow running after it, and a mountain beyond. Oh, and a blue pond, and a lot of little fishes in the pond."

"Kitty, do hear; it don't matter about the clouds," says he.

"But you're not looking. Do look," cried I, rattling as fast as I could speak. "Look, it's the very image of a whale. Can't you see?"

"No," says he, staring; "I don't see no whale, nor anything like a whale. There's only a lot of stupid clouds."

"But clouds are not stupid," said I. "Not stupid at all. The clouds are made of water or snow. Father says so. That's where our water comes from. We should be in a nice taking if we never had any clouds, shouldn't we?" and I laughed at him, and ran up a bank to pick a daisy.

"I don't know anything about the clouds, and I don't care," says Rupert. Which was true of him, and true of thousands, and a most amazing thing it is that men *don't* care to know more about the wonderful things they see every day of their lives. But they don't, and Rupert didn't. "I don't care," says he; "I want to talk about something else—something quite different."

"Then you're not like me, Rupert," I said, sharp enough. "I should like to learn lots of things about the clouds. I want to know what makes them take such pretty shapes, and why the rain stops up there instead of coming down in buckets-

full. And—oh dear, there's one of my pretty roses
falling to bits. Isn't it a pity?"

Rupert wasn't listening. He had on his sort of
bull-dog look, and I knew it meant that he had
made up his mind to say his say, and that say it
he would, no matter all I could do to hinder.

"It's getting late, and I must make haste home,"
says I.

"No, Kitty," says he, and he spoke determined-
like. "You *must* hear me;" and he clutched hold
of my dress with one hand. "There's something
I've got to tell you, and I've been trying the past
month, and can't get it out."

"Then don't get it out now; don't, Rupert," I
said, stopping because I had to stop, for he stood
still. There was nobody but our two selves within
sight. "Don't say it, Rupert," I begged.

"But I must, and will," said he; "I can't wait
no longer. Kitty, there's only one thing in all the
world that I care for, and that is to know—Kitty,
hear me—one moment, Kitty—I want you to
promise that you'll be my wife some day. Won't
you?"

But I snatched my dress from his hand, and set
off running.

"Oh, not yet! not yet!" I cried. I had a sort
of feeling that some day perhaps it might come
about, because I knew father and mother were so
fond of Rupert, and Rupert's mother and sisters
were so fond of me. I didn't know, though,
whether I was willing myself, and anyway I meant

to keep my girlhood a little longer.   " Oh, not yet!
Nothing of that sort yet! " I cried.

Poor Rupert was not the lover I had secretly
pictured to myself.   I suppose most girls have their
little dreams, and I had mine, though I did not
waste time reading trashy tales, like many girls,
for mother never allowed it.   Still I had my little
dream, and there was a hero in the dream,—somebody tall and handsome and straight and nice-
mannered,— not like Rupert, with his round
shoulders, and his shuffling walk, and his slow
speech, and his good plain face.

I did not want to distress him by saying " No,"
outright; and I could not make up my mind to
say " Yes."   So I only called out, " Oh, not yet! "
and ran away.   Rupert did not try to overtake me.

Mother was in-doors, mending a coat of father's,
when I reached home; and standing in the doorway was one of our neighbours, Mrs. Hammond,—
a widow with a lot of children.   She was a hard-
working woman, and deserving in many ways; but
she was a great talker, and mother couldn't bear
her.   If she had not been very good-natured, she
would not often have come to our cottage, for as
sure as ever she came she had a snubbing or a cold
shoulder.

But I liked Mrs. Hammond, because she was
so fond of me.   I think I was ready to like anybody in those days, who would give me love, or
who would even say pretty things.   That's maybe

better than to be of a morose habit, caring for nobody ; but it has its dangers. I had a loving little
heart, and it was easy won, and I was easy led.

When I saw Mrs. Hammond's broad figure in our
doorway, with her short skirt looped up, and the
black strings of her bonnet falling loose, and one
arm held akimbo, as she commonly liked to stand,
I made haste to get in before she should leave, and
as soon as she set eyes on me, she exclaimed,—

" Here comes our village beauty ! "

" Kitty's not such a goose as to believe that,"
mother says, very short.

" It wasn't I who said it first, I can tell you
that," Mrs. Hammond replied. " It was Lady
Arthur."

" Stuff and nonsense ! " says my mother.

" But it was; and I'm telling you the truth.
You don't think I'd make up such a thing, do
you ? " asked Mrs. Hammond.

Sir Richard and Lady Arthur owned the estate,
and spent part of the year at the big house in its
big garden, nearly two miles from the station.
Mrs. Hammond had once been Lady Arthur's maid.
That was many years ago, before Lady Arthur was
married, or Mrs. Hammond either ; but Lady Arthur
was kind to her still, in memory of those days, and
sometimes Mrs. Hammond went to tea with the
servants at the big house.

" It was Lady Arthur, and no mistake," Mrs.
Hammond went on. " The cook told me so herself.
She told me Lady Arthur said one day that your

Kitty was the prettiest and sweetest girl in the village, and the beauty of the place. Cook says Lady Arthur called her, ' Our village beauty.' That's something to blush for, isn't it, Kitty ? "

I suppose I did blush. Mother looked hard at Mrs. Hammond, and then hard at me.

" Kitty has got a pleasant face," she said slowly. " That's not Kitty's doing. It's a gift. I hope she will be thankful for it, as for all other gifts from above. But it won't be a ' sweet ' face long, if she takes to being vain and conceited. There's nothing spoils prettiness like thinking a lot about oneself. And you're doing the best you can to make her."

" Kitty's not going to be vain or conceited," said Mrs. Hammond, who, I think, was as surprised as I was at mother's long speech. " Kitty is going to be her dear little humble self. Why, dear me ! it don't make a girl conceited to be told she's pretty when she *is* pretty. Kitty can't help knowing that, every time she looks in the glass. No good comes of denying that white's white, Mrs. Phrynne."

" Nobody need deny it," mother answered; " and no need to talk about it, neither."

" Maybe not; but all the world can't sit mum, for ever and a day," said Mrs. Hammond, with a laugh. " You don't care about looks, do you, Kitty ?   You're too sensible a girl."

" I don't know," I said. " I shouldn't like to be ugly."

"That's true enough; true of anybody," said Mrs. Hammond, and she laughed again. "Well, you may thank your stars you're *not* ugly."

Mother lifted her head up again to look at Mrs. Hammond. "No," she said; "it's to be hoped Kitty 'll not do anything so foolish. I hope she will thank God for His gifts. The stars haven't much to do with it, anyway."

Mrs. Hammond had had enough, I suppose, for she said good-bye, and went off, beckoning to me to follow. Mother did not try to keep me back.

"Your mother and I don't get along, somehow," Mrs. Hammond said, as we stood together on the gravel path. The flowers were out in bloom all around us—roses, and pinks, and sweet-williams, not in patches of colour, but all mixed up together. Father took such a pride in his garden; the flowers were his friends and his pets. But we were not thinking about flowers just then. "I don't know why, I'm sure," she went on, "only I don't mean any harm. Lots of people say that, and I'm sure I don't know what the sense of it is; so I suppose the words are silly. But, dear me, one can't be always stopping to weigh every word."

I remember that the text about "every idle word" having to be accounted for, rushed straight into my mind.

"But, of course, your mother likes to know you are admired, Kitty," she went on.

"I don't know. I don't think she does," I said.

"Oh, nonsense! She must. Any mother does. She's only afraid of your being hurt, and it's odd she should, such a humble little thing as you are. If you were like some girls, now! But there, you're a pretty little dear, and the beauty of the village, no matter what anybody says. And now, I've got to be off, and not waste any more time."

I did not go in directly. It was almost time for the afternoon express to go by, and I was not in a hurry for what mother might say. Of course, I knew that Mrs. Hammond was not wise to speak to me as she did; but, all the same, I was pleased, and I did not want to be told that Mrs. Hammond was a silly woman, not worth listening to. So I stayed out a little, lingering about in the sunshine. Mother was busy, and I ought to have been helping her; but I never was fond of work, and I knew she would not mind my having a little more fresh air.

The afternoon express was a favourite of mine. I could not have told why, but it always was, and always had been. It did not stop at our station; none of the fast trains did. I always liked to watch it rushing past, and making a whirl of dust and sticks, and a grand commotion. Ever since I was a little child I always had liked to watch that express, and somehow I never grew tired of it. They used to laugh at my fancy. Father and the men got so used to the trains going by that they didn't even hear them, except when there was need of attending to signals. And when I was busy,

I did not hear the other trains either. I never had time to attend to the morning express. The afternoon express came at a time when I was pretty free, and as I say, I had a funny liking for it, almost as if it was a friend of mine.

So I went along the gravel path of our garden that ran parallel with the line, climbing up the gentle slope to the level top of the embankment. The line curved away from our station both ways. The express was to come from the east, on the nearer rails; and there was a pretty sharp ascent going up all the way from our station to the next station in the westerly direction——a sharper ascent than one often sees on a railway. I used often to notice how the trains seemed to labour and drag going that way, and how merrily they would spin down the other way. It made a lot of difference in the amount of coal used.

Well, I reached the end of our little gravel path, walking slowly, with my back to the station, where a gate opened out on a rough path that went along the top of the embankment. I noticed carelessly, as one notices things without much caring, that mother's old red shawl, which father gave her long ago, was lying in a heap on the little bench. Mother must have been out for something with it over her shoulders, for she often felt chilly; and she must have let it drop, and forgotten it.

I went three steps, and picked up the shawl. Then I turned, and looked up and down the rail.

In a moment I saw something which filled me

B

with horror.   Just where I stood, I could see farther along the line, towards the west and south-west, than any one within the station could see.   And my eyes fell upon a big empty truck, slowly running down the nearer rails towards the station—the very rails upon which the express train must almost directly pass.

A little while before, an engine had passed, drawing a large number of empty trucks.   These would, I knew, be put upon a siding at the next station, until the express should have gone by. The hindermost empty truck had plainly broken loose from its couplings, and, after coming to a standstill, had begun to run gently down the slope.

There had been worse than carelessness for such a thing to come about.   A guard's van has to be always at the end of a train ; and for it not to be there is against the law.   But in those days folks weren't so careful nor particular as in these ; and accidents from carelessness do sometimes happen even now.

If the guard's van had been in its right place, such an accident could never have happened unknown to the guard.   The fact was, they had put on two or three empty trucks at the last station before ours, *behind* the guard's van, in a hurry, thinking it would not matter for just two stations, after which they had to shunt.   And here was the consequence !

Nobody had found out yet what had happened. In another half-minute or less it would come within

sight of the men, but that would be too late.   I
knew that the express was close upon due, and it
was always punctual.   If I ran down to the station
to give warning, it would be of no use.   All this
flashed upon me in a moment.   I felt half wild
with the awful horror of what was coming.   For
the express at full speed to dash into the truck must
mean death to many.

For one instant I had a frightened childish im-
pulse to drop down and hide my face, and not see
nor hear anything.   But I did not give in to the
wish.

Something had to be done!   The question was
—what?   I looked at the signal-post—yes, the
arm was down!   The express was coming!

Almost like a voice from heaven, the thought
came spinning through my brain of mother's old
red shawl.

That was enough!   A danger-flag was ready to
hand, and I waited for no more.   Mother's voice
called out to me from the cottage; she said after
that she saw me standing and staring, and so white,
that she thought me struck for illness, and she was
frightened.

But I could not answer or look at her.   I rushed
headlong through the little gate, and along the
path at the top of the embankment, my feet hardly
touching the ground.   I had been a fast runner
at school, and now it seemed as if I were flying.
I got farther in those few seconds than I would
have thought possible; and I was sobbing for

breath, yet still I ran. In those days trains could not be brought to a standstill so quick as they are with the brakes now in use; and all the while the truck was drawing nearer.

There was the train! It seemed to burst upon me all at once, thundering along at an awful pace. And lying a little way ahead was the thing in its path, which meant danger to so many.

Would the driver see me? I felt so small, so puny; and the red shawl was such a little thing to keep off destruction from those scores of people, seated quietly inside, reading, talking, sleeping, little dreaming what threatened them!

I had opened the shawl as I ran, and now I waved it wildly about, jumping up like a mad creature, and doing all I could to draw attention.

In one flash, as it seemed, the train went by. Had they seen me? Had they understood? There were heads enough thrust out of the windows; but how about the two men upon the engine?

That was the most I could do. I felt all at once that I had reached the end of my strength. Everything was spinning, and the rush of the train sounded in the air. I dropped down on my knees, hiding my face in the shawl, sobbing aloud, and stopping my ears; for I could not bear to listen to what might come next.

CHAPTER II.

A GOLD WATCH.

I DO not know how long I crouched down, huddled together on the ground. It could not have been more than two or three minutes: yet it seemed like an hour to me. Though I stopped both ears, I fancied I heard shrieks: and all at once I could bear the suspense no longer. I felt that I must know the worst.

So I stood up without more ado, and walked back as fast as ever I could to the little gate— which was not very fast, for my legs were swaying under me. Though I had run the distance in almost no time, it seemed long as I came back, and I could hardly drag one foot after the other. I was hugging the red shawl tight in my arms still, though I did not know it.

There was no mistake about the cries which I had fancied I heard with my ears stopped. At least, that might have been fancy, yet the cries were real; and not only cries, but a buzz and rush of voices within the station, as if a crowd of people were talking and asking questions together. I saw that the train was at a standstill, and the hind

carriages stood all right upon the rails, not seeming
to be injured. That gave me hope that at all events
the collision had not been a bad one. I could not
see the engine or the foremost carriages yet.

I went straight down through our garden, and
into the station from the back. On my way to the
platform I took a peep into a little waiting-room,
and what I saw stands out always like a picture
before me when I think of that day.

Mother was there, quiet as usual, and she held
in her hand a white handkerchief with red stains.
On the floor, lying flat, was a young woman,
dressed in black—rather young, that is to say,
though not quite a girl, with shut eyes and a white
face, and something red spotting her white lips.
A young man stood close to mother, tall and dark-
haired, and with such a troubled face!—and the
surgeon of Claxton neighbourhood, Mr. Baitson,
knelt on the other side of the young woman, stoop-
ing over her. I could not see what he was doing,
and I did not wait to find out. I had a dread of
the sight of blood, and I fled away at once to the
platform.

The bustle and confusion there were more than
I know how to describe. Everybody seemed to
have leaped out of the train the moment it stopped,
and everybody was talking. Some were asking
questions, and some were angry, and two or three
ladies were half fainting, and one was in a fit of
shrieking hysterics, with a lot of folks round her.
Perhaps she had been so taken by surprise that she

could not control herself ; but yet I think she need not have screamed so loud.

Nobody noticed me at first, and I stepped into the corner beside the big station-clock, where I stood, quaking still, and glad to lean against the wall.

The engine and truck had met before the train came to a standstill, for the truck was turned half over, twisted round, and thrown partly off the rails. The shock must have been sharp enough to do some damage, and yet it could not be called much of a collision, compared with what it might have been. Strange to say, neither the engine nor any of the carriages had left the rails ; and nobody seemed to be much hurt except the one passenger in the waiting-room.

One very stout person near me had put himself into a tremendous rage. He stamped his foot, and was as red as fire ; and he stormed at everybody all round in a perfect fury. " It was scandalous ! —disgraceful !—atrocious ! " he shouted. " Atrocious ! disgraceful ! scandalous ! " He said those words over and over, till I never could hear them since without remembering him.

I was innocent enough to think that he must be some very important man, he made such a fuss. But I might have known better. I learnt later that he was a rich butcher from the next town, who had made his fortune and retired from business. There was a quiet little grey-haired gentleman, going about in the crowd, asking one and another in a soft voice who was hurt; and I never should have guessed him to be an Earl, but he was. The butcher did scolding enough for him and every one. Then I saw Sir Richard Arthur, and our clergyman, Mr. Armstrong, and a stranger, all three talking with my father in a little group, near to me. Poor father looked terribly pale, as well he might, and Sir Richard was pale too. The stranger was a brother of Sir Richard's, I soon found, and was one of the Company's directors, travelling by that train. I heard him say to Mr. Armstrong—

"But who waved the signal which has saved our lives?"

"Nobody seems to know," was the answer.

Mr. Armstrong was an elderly man, with grey hair and a kind face. He had been Rector in Claxton for many years, and he was like a father to the whole village. As he spoke his eyes fell on me, shrinking into the shadow of the clock, and he said "Kitty!" in a surprised tone.

"Kitty!" my father echoed, and they all turned. I don't know how it was they guessed the truth at once, but somehow they did. Perhaps it was the red shawl, which I held so fast; perhaps that I was panting still with my run and the fright.

Mr. Armstrong put a hand on my arm, and drew me forward. Rupert told others afterwards that I had my eyes wide open, so as to seem twice their usual size, with a fixed stare like one terror-struck; and no colour was in my cheeks; and my hat had fallen off; and the red shawl was rolled up tight in my arms. I did not see Rupert, but he had that minute found me out.

Father pointed to the shawl, and said again—"Kitty!" He seemed as if he could not say anything else.

, "Kitty, my dear, was it you who gave warning?" Mr. Armstrong asked in his fatherly way.

"I saw the truck—" I tried to answer; but my voice sounded queer, and the words would not come rightly. I could not think what was the matter, and I cried "Father!" in a fright.

Somebody handed Mr. Armstrong a glass of water, and he put it to my lips. That took away the parched feeling, and then Rupert came near, and mustered courage to say in his blunt fashion, —"Kitty did it. I saw her on the top of the embankment, running like a hare. I didn't know what for."

"Was it you, Kitty?" father asked.

"I saw the truck," I said; "and I had mother's shawl; and I ran to meet the express. There wasn't time for anything else."

"Brave girl!" "Splendid presence of mind!" I heard them say. Other people came, and the crowd round us grew, and there was a buzz of voices, asking and exclaiming and praising. Sir Richard shook hands with me, and his brother, the director, followed his example, saying, "No doubt many of us owe our lives to this little girl's promptitude." I don't suppose he took me for seventeen.

By that time I had colour enough, and I felt
almost as if I could sink into the ground; yet I
liked it all, and the words of praise set me into a
glow of happiness; for it did seem grand to think
that I, little Kitty Phrynne, should have been able
to save lives.

Somebody spoke about "wretched mismanage-
ment," and "arrant carelessness." And that of
course was true enough, though it wasn't to do
with us at Claxton, for the luggage train hadn't
even stopped at our station. But father and the
men had noticed the trucks put on behind the
guard's van; and there was a lot of talk about this.
I heard the word "illegal" over and over again
from the gentlemen, and Mr. Arthur frowned, and
said somebody would have to be called to account
for that!—which indeed did happen, and more
than one man was dismissed, though nobody to do
with us.

Then there was some wondering why the truck
hadn't been seen sooner, and I thought poor father
was being blamed. I said, "O no!" and explained to them how we could see farther along
the curve from the top of our garden than from
anywhere else near. It was just that one chance
glimpse, if one may use the word "chance" in such
a manner, which gave me power to act. The truck
was seen from the station almost directly after;
and a telegram came from the next station, warning us that it had been missed. But all would
have been too late if I had not had that glimpse.

After this more was said about me. Such a
fuss was made, that it wouldn't be much wonder
if my head was a little turned. Mr. Armstrong
said to me in a low voice, "Kitty, this is something to thank God for!" But I am afraid I
thought more about being praised by men than
about thanking God. And yet there was nothing
in what I did that deserved praise. If it hadn't
been for that Heaven-sent thought about the red
shawl—which I am quite sure *was* Heaven-sent,
and not my own—the crash must have taken
place.

Then mother came out of the waiting-room where
she had been all this while. She did not seem
flurried, but faced the crowd of gentlemen as
quietly as she would have faced her own husband
alone. Mother was not one to be easily upset.

It took her by surprise to find Sir Richard
shaking hands with her and congratulating, and
Mr. Arthur following his example again, and me
looking red and bashful and happy, and a lot of
people asking, "Is this her mother?" and pressing
round with kind speeches about what they owed
to me.

Mother stood still, looking from one to another
with her sharp quiet eyes: not flurried, you know,
but waiting to take in the meaning of things.
When she began to understand, she said, "That's
what the child was after, is it?" She made her
courtesy to Sir Richard, for mother was never
above courtesying, like some silly folks. She'd

always pay honour where honour was due, and she was respectful to everybody: the consequence of which was that she always had proper honour and respect paid her again. So she courtesied, and said, " Thank you, sir," says she; " I'm very much obliged to you, and I'm glad Kitty had the sense to do her duty."

There was a sort of little fluster at this among the gentlemen. One or two smiled, but most of them only looked pleased, and the quiet little gentle-mannered man, whom I didn't know to be an Earl, came forward and said in a sort of approving kind of way, as if he was used to have his opinion thought of,—

" Quite right! quite right! she did her duty!"

" Yes, sir," mother answered. Then mother looked straight at the Earl, and seemed to know in a moment that he was something out of the common, for she dropped a deeper courtesy to him than to Sir Richard. Mother was always so wonderful knowing about people.

The Earl smiled at mother, as if he understood her a deal better than people generally did, and he held out a soft hand to grasp mother's, which was as clean as his, but not soft, because of the hard work it had to do. " A girl who will do her duty at such a moment speaks well for the mother who has trained her," says he. " What is the little girl's name?" I suppose he called me "little girl" because Mr. Arthur had done so. " Kitty— Kitty what? Kitty Phrynne! I should like to

give Kitty Phrynne a remembrance of the day
when she—did her duty!" The Earl stopped and
smiled before the last three words. (" If everybody
did his duty always, the world would be a different
world from what it is now,') says he.

Then he took out of his pocket a gold watch,
with a short gold chain hanging to it, and put
both into my hand. "I hope you will always be
brave and true, and will always do your duty," he
said. "I want you to keep this as a little token
of gratitude from Lord Leigh, and in remembrance
of the day when your prompt action saved many
lives."

It was quite a bit of a speech, and one gentleman called "Hear! hear!" and others clapped
their hands. I don't know what I said or did,
for I was all in a whirl. It isn't every girl of
seventeen who has a gold watch and chain given
her by a real Earl. Rupert says I made a courtesy like mother, and dropped my eyes in the prettiest
way,—I mean he said so after. But Rupert was
no judge, poor fellow, in those days, because he
admired everything that I did.

I heard the buzz all round, which sounded as
if everybody was pleased, and I know mother
courtesied again and said, " I'm very much obliged
to your Lordship," or something like that. Then
she turned to me, and said in just exactly her
usual tone :—

"There's hot water wanted presently, Kitty,
and a bed in the parlour for somebody that's hurt.

We're going to take her in and do for her. The spare bed, you know. Run home and get things ready."

"Quite a character!" I heard Mr. Arthur say very low, as if he was speaking to himself; and the Earl smiled again, and said, as if he didn't mind being heard—"That is the training which has saved our lives to-day."

When mother said a thing was to be done, I knew she meant it, sharp! So off I went, not waiting a moment, though I shouldn't have minded staying for a few more words of praise. I did just hear, as I passed, somebody say, "That's a charming little maid!" and Sir Richard replied, "My wife calls her 'our village beauty.'" So Mrs. Hammond had spoken truth; and if my head wasn't turned already it had a chance of being so then.

Before so many listeners I was too shy to ask mother what she meant about our taking somebody in; and indeed I felt pretty sure it must be the young woman in the waiting-room.

Our cottage wasn't very big. On the ground floor there was the parlour, which we did not commonly use, and the kitchen and scullery; and overhead there were father and mother's room, and my room, and a tiny slip of a room besides, with hardly any window and no fireplace, and only space for a bed and chair and washstand. We had a friend to sleep there once in a way, but it wouldn't have done for a sick person; and our crooked stairs were bad for carrying anybody up. Two years before, we had taken in father's mother for a time till she died; and, because she was infirm, the bed and things from this slip-room were put into the parlour for her use. I knew that was what mother meant me to do now; and I did not quite see how I was to get the bed down by myself.

However, I knew mother wished me to set to work at once, asking no questions. So I put the kettle on the kitchen fire to boil, and then ran upstairs. I stopped for one moment on the landing, to look at the beautiful watch that I still held, with its gold face and handsome chased back, and the solid gold chain hanging to it. I could hardly believe they were really mine, my very own. It seemed such a strange thing to have happened.

But there was no time to stand and think; so I put away the watch in a drawer, under my clothes, and ran to the little slip-room. The first thing was to carry down some of the bedding, and the wash-handstand set. I could manage those, and the wash-handstand itself, which was light. Then I took the pillows and blankets, and rolled down the thin top mattress, the other having to wait for help; and next I began taking the iron bed to pieces. I was used to all these things, only I never had been strong at lifting.

Presently I could hear Rupert's voice calling from below.

"Kitty!" says he, "your mother says you'll want help."

"I've got to get this bed down, and I can't do it all alone," I said.

"No, I should think not—a little thing like you!" he says, clumping up the stairs. "Yes, the bed has to go down. There's a Miss Russell badly hurt—been ill before, I believe—and the shock made her ill again. I don't know more; only they daren't move her more than need be; so your mother's offered to take her in here. Dear me, you've done a lot already!" And he stood still to look. "How ever came you to think of that shawl, Kitty?"

"Why, I had it in my arms," I said. "Come, you'd better be sharp, Rupert. How soon is Miss Russell to be here?"

"As soon as the room's ready. They're in a hurry, I can tell you. I couldn't get away sooner, for everybody was wanted to clear the line."

"Is it done now?" I asked, as he got up a great, bundle of the iron pieces of the bed, and let them fall with a tremendous clatter. "Oh, Rupert!" I said, putting my hands to my ears.

"Couldn't help it," said he. "Yes, it's all done. Express off directly."

"And everybody going on?"

"Except those that meant to stay, and Miss Russell and her brother. Wish he was going too!" I heard Rupert mutter; and I asked—

"Is that the brother who was with her in the waiting-room—tall and nice-looking?" I'm afraid I said this to tease Rupert.

"That's the young puppy," he said gruffly; and he marched out of the room.

"Where is he going to sleep?" I asked, following Rupert with more pieces of the bed.

"Don't know and don't care! Not here!" said Rupert, still more gruffly.

When we got downstairs, he went up again, but he wouldn't let me go too. He said I was tired, and I had better stay where I was. In a few minutes he was putting the bedstead together in the corner I chose. Then he brought the mattress, and to save time, I let him help me make the bed, though he was clumsy enough at it. He looked glum too, and as if his mind wasn't on what he had to do.

"Nobody else hurt except Miss Russell?" I asked presently.

"Nothing to speak of, except the stoker, and he's able to go on. It's a wonder there wasn't a lot killed. Your father looks bad still. I say, you spoke up bold for him, Kitty!"

"Why shouldn't I?" I asked.

"I don't know. I didn't suppose it was *in* you," says he. "And they liked you all the better for it too. I could see that."

Then he told me that the Earl was a relation to Lady Arthur—uncle, I think—and that Mr. Arthur was come to stop for a night or two at the big house. And then I told him he had better take word the room was ready.

In a few minutes I saw them coming; the poor thing laid on a shutter, which father and Rupert and one of the porters and her brother were carrying. They moved slowly, and mother came on first.

"Room all straight, Kitty ? " says she.

" Yes, mother," I said. " What is the matter with her ? "

" It's what they call ' hæmorrhage,' " mother said. " Bleeding from inside, you know; and very bad. She had it once before, and the shock brought it on again."

" And nobody else hurt ? " I said.

" She and her brother was in the front carriage, close to the engine," mother said. " And she was going backwards : so I suppose she came in for more of a jar."

" Is the bleeding over now, mother ? "

" If it don't come on again ! That's the fear ! The doctor's afraid of the least movement. That's why I offered to have her in here."

Then I saw Mr. Baitson following with Mr. Armstrong; but I did not look at them much, for my eyes were soon chained to Miss Russell's face.

I had never seen any one like her before. It wasn't that she was pretty. I shouldn't wonder if she never had been exactly pretty; and she was past girlhood then, with a few grey hairs showing.

But there was a wonderful quiet in the face, like the quiet of the sea on a still day; and when she opened her eyes they were full of gentle goodness.

"Hush, not a word!" Mr. Baitson said, when she wanted to speak.

She smiled and gave in directly; but her eyes wandered round till they fell on her brother.

He looked sorely troubled, and I think his sister noticed this, for she kept watching him as long as he was within sight. When they had laid her on the bed, only Mr. Baitson stayed, beside mother and me. He said she was to have her clothes slipped off her with the least possible movement, and he would call again by-and-by. Then I saw Miss Russell sign to him to go close, and she whispered, "Walter!"

"You want to see your brother? Well, just for a moment. But I can't have talking, you know," said Mr. Baitson.

The brother didn't so much as give a glance towards mother or me when he was called in. He went straight to the bed and bent down, and I heard a sort of choke, as if he was almost crying, and then a sound like a word which I couldn't make out.

"Forgive you, yes!" she said tenderly, and her hand went over his hair. "My own boy!"

"Hush! this won't do!" Mr. Baitson said almost sternly.

She gave him a look as much as to say, "I forgot!" and Mr. Baitson hurried the young man off.

Mother managed the undressing beautifully. I

had to stay, and do as I was told ; and all the time
I was in a foolish fright lest the bleeding should
begin again. Foolish and selfish too: for I was
frightened chiefly, or at least partly, on my own
account. But I didn't say anything, for mother
would never tamely give in, either with herself
or anybody else, to any sort of feelings or fancies
which might hinder one from doing one's duty.
She knew I was a bit of a coward naturally, and
she often said she wouldn't have me grow up a
silly useless woman, running away from people
when they most needed me. I would have run
away that day, if I had had my will; for I had a
sick horror of the sight of blood. But I am sure
I have been thankful enough in years since that
mother made me fight the weakness, and not become
a slave to it.

Well, the poor thing was settled at last, lying in
one of mother's nice frilled night-dresses, her hands
folded on the white counterpane, and her eyes shut.
The brown hair with its grey streaks was in one
loose plait,—she had a lot of hair, and after all
there wasn't much grey in it,—and she looked
younger than when I saw her first. I made up my
mind that she couldn't at the most be much over
thirty, and I wasn't wrong. But thirty sounded
middle-aged to me at seventeen.

Mother was a first-rate nurse, though she never
had a hospital-training. It seemed to come natural-
like to her, as it does to some people ; and she had
had practice. So she made up her mind to do the

nursing herself, at least for the first few days, till we saw what would be wanted.

That meant that I should have to do most of the cooking and the cleaning. I was not best pleased with the thought; for though mother had trained me to all sorts of work, yet I was used to having a good deal of time to myself. But here again I knew I should have to buckle-to, and not to think of my own fancies. Mother would not let me overdo myself, I might be sure, yet she wouldn't allow any laziness.

Presently she sent me to get the tea ready. It had been put off late through all that had happened; and she was sure father and I must want it.

When I got into the kitchen, I found father there talking to Miss Russell's brother, who looked miserable still; though for all that I couldn't help noticing how handsome he was, with his black hair and black eyes, and a sort of manner that was just the opposite of Rupert's rough ways, and almost like the manner of a gentleman. At least, I thought so then.

He and father were speaking softly, so as not to disturb the poor sick sister, and neither of them paid any attention to me coming in. Father had laid the table, and put the kettle on again to boil; so I made the tea without a word.

Then of a sudden father turned towards me, and says—"Mr. Russell will take tea with us, Kitty." And he said to Mr. Russell—"That's my brave little girl who gave the warning."

"I don't think I was brave, father," I said. "It only came into my head."

"It wouldn't have come into everybody's head, though," Mr. Russell said.

He had been as dismal as could be, up to that moment, in a sort of limp way, the corners of his mouth dropping, with a look as if nothing in the world could comfort him. But the dismalness began to go off with his first cup of tea. He sat upright, and I felt him looking at me, in the way strangers often did look: for those were my pretty days, and it's no use denying that I was an uncommonly pretty girl. Everybody said so, and I suppose everybody must have known. I was used to being admired, but still it made me blush.

Father was pale still, and I was glad to see him taking something. Then I went to ask mother if I should stay in her place a few minutes, though I was quaking inwardly at the idea, for I knew that the dreadful bleeding might come on again any moment. It was a braver thing of me, really, to offer to do this, than it had been to wave the red shawl, though of course nobody guessed it. But mother said she had promised the doctor not to leave Miss Russell until he came again: so I carried in some tea to her.

Mr. Russell would persist in helping me. I had to let him bring the tray across the passage to the door of the room, where his sister was.

I thought that uncommon pretty, and nice of him too. It seemed fine to be waited on by Mr.

Russell, in the sort of way that I knew gentlemen
waited on ladies in grand houses. I had seen it
for myself at the big house, when I went there to
help for a week, one of the housemaids being taken
suddenly ill. The servants all made a pet of me,
and the ladies too, and I was sent in and out of the
drawing-room with messages.

I had seen the gentlemen picking up what the
ladies dropped, and fetching what they wanted,
and carrying what they had to take anywhere, and
so on. Mother said it was always like that with
real gentlemen.

But I didn't see, and I never do see, why things
shouldn't be something like that too, in the homes
of working-men. Because a man is a working-man,
and wears rough clothes, that's no reason why he
must be gruff and short. The Bible command, "Be
courteous," is meant for everybody alike—not for
gentlefolk only.

To be sure I've known many a working-man
who wasn't exactly gruff or short, and who was
always kind; and yet it would never come into
their heads to do that sort of little polite thing,
just because they were not trained to it, you know.
I suppose they would have laughed at the idea
outright; though I don't know why they should,
except that Englishmen always laugh at what they
are not used to.

I'm quite sure of one thing, and that is that the
more gentle-mannered and attentive a man is to his
women-folk, the more they'll slave their lives out

for him.   Scolding and gruff words don't bring but
only a sullen sort of service; and there's too many
a husband and father who seldom troubles himself
to speak in his home at all, except in some sort of
a grumble.

But then of course there's another side to the
matter.   If the husbands have got to be polite and
gentle to their wives, the wives have got to be
polite and gentle to their husbands.   I *have* known
wives who'd speak to their husbands in a tone like
the screech of an engine-whistle.   And that, to say
the least of the matter, isn't pretty !

Well,—to come back to our tea that afternoon !

Unhappy as Mr. Russell was, he managed to eat
plenty.   He said he had never in his life tasted
such bread as ours, and he praised our milk and
our butter and the jam, as if he hadn't had food
worth eating before.   I thought it kind of him;
though to be sure I never do hold with a lot of
talking about the food we eat.   It's right to be
thankful for nice things, but there's plenty that's
better worth talking about than eatables.

He told us next a few things about himself and
his sister.

They had been orphans since his boyhood; and
they had no near relations in the world.   She was
like a mother to him always.   Till lately they had
lived in Bristol ; but at that time Mr. Russell was
schoolmaster in a National School at Littleburgh,
which was a small manufacturing town at no great
distance from Claxton — an hour or so by rail.

His sister took in dressmaking, for she was a capital worker, clever with her fingers. But she hadn't so much work yet at Littleburgh, where they were almost strangers, as in Bristol, where they had had many friends.

I thought it so good of her to leave all her friends, that she might make a home for him in a new place. When I said so, he said, "Ah, yes, just like Mary, poor dear!"

One or two things that he let drop made me fancy they or their parents must have known better times. At all events, I felt sure he was very superior and very clever. If not, how could he have been a schoolmaster? That gave me a sort of respect for him.

He said his sister had taken care he should have a good education, and he spoke so nicely and feelingly about repaying what he owed to her. A time would come, he said,—perhaps soon,—when she would not need to work, but would only depend upon him. I couldn't help thinking what a good brother he must be!

CHAPTER III.

TWO OF THEM.

TALKING to father and me, Mr. Russell grew lively; and once mother came to the kitchen door, with her finger up, and a " Hush ! " for Mr. Russell had raised his voice too much. I wondered a little that he could forget so soon, when he was so fond of his sister. And yet I liked him. I could not help liking him.

Now and then he seemed quite young; and then, again, he spoke as if he was older. I was puzzled; but after a time he told us he was twenty-four, and his sister was thirty-two; so that settled the matter.

" She's a good sister to me—always has been. I shouldn't think a chap ever had a better sister," he said, and a sort of cloud came over his face, as if all at once he remembered something that he had managed to forget.

" Then I hope you're a good brother to her," father said.

Mr. Russell sighed at this, and looked melancholy, but he didn't explain why, nor answer what father said.

48

Then father had to go back into the station, for
a train was nearly due; and I could see he wanted
to take Mr. Russell with him, while Mr. Russell
wasn't at all in haste to go.

Perhaps that was natural enough, his sister being
ill in our cottage, and he having no other home in
the place.

He was to sleep, I had found, at Mrs. Bowman's.
For Mrs. Bowman had a spare room, and was glad
any time of a lodger. That would be cheaper than
going to the inn; and it was plain they had to think
about expenses.

I wondered how Rupert would like him being
there.

Father offered to point out the way to Mrs.
Bowman's, and Mr. Russell said, " Yes—presently;
but might he have just one more cup of tea first ? "
So father had to go off, leaving him and me together. I didn't think he half liked it, though
mother was close by, just across the passage.
Father was always so careful of his " little wild
rose," as he called me; and of course he didn't
know anything much of Mr. Russell yet.

I poured out the tea for Mr. Russell, and then
waited for him to finish, getting out the grey sock
which I was knitting at odd times for my father.
Mother never liked to see me nor anybody sitting
idle. She always said tongues went faster when
fingers went slower; and, to be sure, I didn't get
as much work done as I might, when I was set off
talking.

Mr. Russell seemed in no haste to be done. He sipped his tea, and set it down to cool. Then he leaned back, looking melancholy again, and said, " Poor Mary ! The best of sisters ! "

"I am sure, from her face, she is good," I said.

" She is *too* good," said Mr. Russell, with a sort of smile which I didn't understand.

" I don't see how anybody can be too good," I said, and I spoke timidly, for I thought Mr. Russell wonderfully clever.

" There are different kinds of goodness," says Mr. Russell ; and that was a new notion to me. I couldn't think what he meant ; for, to be sure, the Bible don't tell of two kinds.

" I should think your sister's was the right kind," I said.

" Well—yes," says he. " I didn't mean a ' wrong ' kind, you see, when I spoke of different kinds. I only meant that people might be good in too exalted a way for everyday life. That is Mary's tendency, perhaps. Poor dear Mary ! " He sighed again, and then he reached out his cup, saying, " *Might* he have a little more sugar ? "

I couldn't help a sort of amused feeling at his being able to think about sugar ; and yet I was half vexed with myself for being amused. After all, it takes a lot of trouble to bring a man to such a pass that he don't care what he eats or drinks. Women mostly come to that point sooner ; and yet not women of the weak and faddy sort ; for the worse trouble they are in, the more faddy and complaining they get.

Mr. Russell helped himself to the sugar, and then he stirred his tea round and round with the spoon, till it got to look like a whirlpool with a hole in the middle. Presently he sipped it again, and told me it was "perfect," and after that he went on with what he was saying.

"Yes, Mary is a most excellent creature—too good for common life. One can't help admiring, of course—but still——" and he shook his head, as much as to say that it wouldn't do, wouldn't do at all!

"Perhaps it would be better if everybody was the same," I said, thinking how father would speak and how mother would look in my place. I felt that there was something out of joint in what he was saying; and yet I did not want to feel anything that was not in his favour.

"The world would be at a standstill," says he. "People must have common sense if they are to get on in life."

I didn't know what he meant then; I know better now. He meant that we had to serve Mammon as well as God; and that, in matters of business, Mammon must come first, God second. He would not have put it so plain as that, of course, but it came to nothing less. Yes, and it always does end in that, when we try to do what our Lord said couldn't be done—when we try to serve Mammon and God too. Mr. Russell's

"Mammon" was "getting on in life," and making money. He wouldn't put the service of God before that, and his sister *would*. That was why he called her "too good" for common life. But perhaps I ought not to say all this now. Perhaps I ought to leave it to be found out later.

Mr. Russell all at once turned the talk to something different.

"By-the-bye," said he, "I'm told the Earl gave you his own watch and chain."

"Yes," I said, and I got rather red.

"I don't wonder your father is proud."

"Was he proud about it?" I said. "Then he didn't show what he felt."

"Might I," Mr. Russell went on—"might I see the watch?"

I didn't see how to refuse or why I need: so I ran upstairs and brought down the gold watch and chain, laying them on the table in front of Mr. Russell. He took them up and examined both closely, letting his tea get cold, he was so interested.

"You'll have to mind you keep them in a safe place," he said after a while. "The Earl knows how to do things in a princely style. You're in luck, I can tell you. It's a thirty-guinea watch if it's worth a penny, and the chain half as much again!"

I was rather startled to hear this.

"First-rate article," says Mr. Russell. "Look, here's where you wind up." I came nearer to be

" He put down the watch and tilted his chair, leaning back on it."—*Page* 47

shown, and at the sound of a step outside the
window he just lifted his eyes for a moment, and
asked in a careless way, "Who is that gawky
young fellow? I saw him at the station."

"Oh, that is Rupert Bowman, our ticket-collector," I said, foolishly ashamed that anybody so plain
and awkward should be a friend of ours.

Rupert walked straight in at the open door, as
he always did. When he saw Mr. Russell sitting
at our table, holding the gold watch, and me
standing near, his face grew as black as midnight.
He scowled at Mr. Russell, and shuffled more than
ever.

What a contrast the two were, to be sure!

"I say, Kitty——" he burst out.

Then he stopped. I knew · why. I didn't
like him to speak so to me before Mr. Russell.
It sounded rude; and, besides, I did not like him
to seem so much at home—calling me by my
name, and putting on that angry manner, as if I
was a child to be scolded! Well, I was but a
silly lass, and my head had been pretty well turned
that day.

I suppose I showed pretty plainly what I thought.
Rupert always said I could toss my head, and could
be scornful, for all I was so humble and bashful.
Not that I was humble really, only folks said it
of me.

Mr. Russell showed plainly what he felt too.
He put down the watch and tilted his chair, leaning back on it, and he fixed his eyes hard upon

Rupert, lifting his eyebrows with a sort of disdain, as if he was looking down upon a lower animal altogether.

I don't now think that kind of manner from one man to another anything grand, and I know well enough it is not gentlemanly. A true gentleman is kind and courteous all round, just as much to those beneath him as to those above him.

But I had seen then very little of life, and Mr. Russell's manner seemed to me uncommon fine and dignified. I grew more and more ashamed to think how awkward and clumsy Rupert was, and how that very day he had dared to ask me to marry him.

I began to feel, too, that I never could nor would marry Rupert,—no, not if he asked me fifty times!

Rupert turned away from me and glared at Mr. Russell. I don't think "glared" is too hard a word. Rupert had a temper naturally, and sometimes it got the better of him, though he did fight to keep it down. Mr. Russell's manner was enough to try it; and Rupert always had cared for me as he cared for nobody else. I suppose it was hard for him to see me with this stranger, so different from himself, and me seeming already taken with him.

"Mr. Phrynne told me I was to show you the way to our cottage," he says in a short angry tone.

"Thank you," Mr. Russell made answer. "When I'm in want of a conductor, I'll apply to you."

It didn't strike me at the moment, that this was

not the way he ought to have taken my father's message.

"Mr. Phrynne said so," Rupert said again gruffly.

"You can be so good as to tell Mr. Phrynne that I already know the way," Mr. Russell answered. "When I have had a stroll, I shall make my appearance at your mother's." Then he turned to me, speaking in a different tone, like to an equal, while his manner to Rupert was like an inferior. "I have kept you too long, I'm afraid," says he; "but I suppose I may look in again by-and-by, just to ask after my poor sister?"

Rupert stood and glared at him still. Mr. Russell didn't seem disturbed. He lifted his cup to drink off the rest of his tea, and I remember how he stuck out his little finger as he held the cup, in a way I thought elegant then, though now I can see it was affected. Isn't it odd, the little stupid things that come back to one's mind, years after, when much more important things are forgotten? Everything that happened on that day is clear to me still, just as if I had pictures of it all laid up in my mind.

Mr. Russell got up to go, and as he gave back the watch to me, he said in an undertone—

"What could your father have meant?—sending such a chap as that!"

Rupert must have heard; he could not help hearing. He stood like a stock till Mr. Russell was gone, and then he turned sharp round upon me, and said—

"You ought to know better, Kitty!"

"Oh, ought I?" said I, getting very red. And of course, it wasn't the way for Rupert to speak to me. He had no business to call me to account in any such tone. But it didn't improve matters for me to be angry. I've often thought since that it was one of the times for mother's favourite saying. Less hot words would have been sooner mended. But we were both young and impatient.

"Oh, ought I?" says I. "I think *you* ought to know better by this time, and not behave as if you'd never learnt any manners."

"How do I behave?" Rupert asked in a fierce way.

"Treating me like a child!" I said. "I'm not a child any longer, and it's time you should know it. And standing staring at Mr. Russell as if you were out of your wits!"

"That—puppy!" said he, and the words came in a smothered fury, not against me but against Mr. Russell. I think he was angry with me too, though only a sort of dull sore anger. "How much do you know about that—puppy!—eh, Kitty?— with his airs and graces! And nobody in the village ever set eyes on him nor heard of him till to-day!"

"I know more than you do," I said. "Calling him names won't make me think any worse of him nor any better of you."

"That's not calling him names. He *is* a puppy," says Rupert. "With his oiled hair and his put-on

manners and his conceit! D'you think I don't
know his sort at first sight?"

" I wish you were half as much a gentleman as
Mr. Russell," I said.

" A gentleman!" Rupert burst into a grating
laugh, as if he felt choked. " Call that a gentleman?"

" Much more of one than you, at any rate," I said.

" I'm not a gentleman, and don't pretend to be;
don't want to be, neither. A man's capable of
being honest, I hope, without using hairdresser's
scent and wearing kid gloves. That's what Mr.
Russell's gentlemanliness means—nothing more and
nothing less. Hairdresser's scent won't stand in the
place of honesty, nor kid gloves in the place of—
of——" Rupert's voice shook, and he could hardly
get out the words—" of real true love, Kitty." He
came a step nearer, looking hard at me. " Kitty,
don't you be taken in!" says he. " Say you
won't!"

" I shall not say anything of the sort," I said,
and I tossed my head, for I could not get over the
way he had spoken to me. " It's no business of
yours!"

" No business of mine who you care for? You
don't mean that!" said he.

" Yes, I do. It's no business of yours at all,"
I said. I'd never spoken so to Rupert before, but
the doings of that day seemed to have changed me
somehow. " I shall care for who I choose," I went
on, " and not ask your leave   And if you mean

to plague me like this, why I shall think better of
Mr. Russell than of you. He does know how to
behave, and you don't."

Such a pity to say so much, wasn't it? What
was the good? I might just as well have held my
tongue. Of course, if I could not marry him, the
sooner I made him understand, the better. But
there's different ways of making folks understand;
and words spoken in a pet are never the right sort.

"You don't like him best, now, Kitty!—say you
don't!" begged Rupert.

I got up and turned short off, as if I was tired
of the talk. If only I had got tired and run away
sooner!

"Say you don't," begged Rupert again. "Kitty,
I'll be as civil to him as ever you can wish, if only
you'll just say you don't, nor won't, like him better
than me."

But I was vexed still, and I said—

"Why shouldn't I? You are so disagreeable,
Rupert. I like Mr. Russell *much* the best."

Rupert looked like somebody who has had a
sharp blow in the face. His eyes grew dull, and
he went slowly out of the kitchen without another
word. I turned my head to see him go, half
minded to call him back,—and there was Mrs.
Hammond in the doorway.

"That's right, Kitty," says she, laughing.
"Keep the young fellows in their place, and don't
you be put upon."

Seeing Mrs. Hammond frightened me, for I

knew that whatever came to her knowledge was sure to be over the whole place. She couldn't keep a thing to herself; and that was partly why mother distrusted her. I did wish I had not said so much. I felt that I wouldn't on any account have others know what I had said to Rupert about liking Mr. Russell. I made light of it all to Mrs. Hammond, and at the same time begged her not to repeat what she'd heard. Mrs. Hammond promised fast enough; but I might have known what the promise was worth.

Then she asked how Miss Russell was, and wanted to see my watch and chain. She had heard all about what had gone on at the station from Mabel Bowman, who was told everything by Rupert himself. That was how I knew that he was the first to see me standing by the clock, and how he had watched me come forward with such wide-open eyes.

While I listened to Mrs. Hammond I was sorry I had been so sharp upon Rupert; and yet, when I thought how he had spoken to me, I was as vexed as ever again.

. . . .

Things went on the next few days as they had begun. Rupert scarcely ever came near, and when he did, if Mr. Russell was by, I felt ashamed again of his plain face and awkward ways. And I liked to know that Mr. Russell admired me.

Mrs. Hammond told me one day I ought to marry a gentleman; and it pleased me to hear her say it, even though I guessed she meant Mr. Russell—and I knew he wasn't a real gentleman.

Mother was very busy with Miss Russell. It didn't seem as if she could know much of what was going on outside the sick-room, she was so much shut up in it. I never could be sure, though. Mother had such sharp eyes; she seemed able to see through anything. Her not speaking meant nothing, for she wasn't a sieve, like many women, always letting everything in her mind run out. If she didn't think the time was come for speaking, she'd wait till it did come.

Miss Russell was very ill for several days. She had to keep still, and at first she might not talk. Mother seldom left her. I think those two took to one another at first sight, as people sometimes do.

She was wonderfully patient, and never complained. She didn't even seem to be in a hurry to get well. I used to go and sit by her sometimes, and watch her quiet pale face. Often she looked as if she had very happy thoughts; but that wasn't always.

One evening, mother had gone for a few minutes into the garden, and I was there instead. Miss Russell was asleep, when all of a sudden she stirred, and put out both hands.

"Don't, don't! oh, Walter, don't!" she says, in such a sad voice.

I kept still, and didn't speak, only wondering what she meant.

"O Walter, don't!" she said again, and then she woke, and her eyes met mine.

"I think you were dreaming, weren't you?" I said.

"Yes, I was dreaming," she said, and sighed. "Such an uncomfortable dream! I am glad you roused me."

I had not roused her, but that did not matter, and I only asked—

"What was the dream about?"

"You, partly," she said, with a little smile.

I was puzzled, thinking how she had called to her brother; but, of course, she did not know me to have heard that.

"What about me?" I asked.

"Nothing much. A foolish dream," said she. "I hope it will never come true. I only dreamt you were going to make a very unhappy marriage, and I was trying to prevent it." She looked at me earnestly, and said, "Not likely to come true, I think. You have been brought up so well and sensibly. Kitty——" and she stopped—"Kitty, you are a very pretty girl. You can't help knowing it. Don't you marry the first foolish young fellow who is ready to run after you just because of your pretty face. That wouldn't mean being happy."

Mother came in and put a stop to the talking. I could see she was not pleased with me for letting Miss Russell say so much. She had heard our voices going, and that brought her back.

Miss Russell was allowed to see her brother once or twice a day, for just five minutes. It always seemed to me those visits did her no good. She used to look so worried after, in her quiet way. Yet I could not find out why.

We had learnt that the two were off together for a fortnight's outing; and I shouldn't think they could well afford the expense, from little remarks that were made. There had been some sort of crank in the plan. Miss Russell said one day, " Walter was bent on it ! " And another day Mr. Russell said, " Poor dear Mary was so set on it ! " Between them I was puzzled. I felt sure Miss Russell must have been in the right, and tried to feel sure Mr. Russell couldn't have been in the wrong.

He was in and out of our cottage a great deal, —more than father and mother liked, I am sure, though I don't think they knew quite how often he came, and I suppose they hardly knew how to stop his coming. It was so natural that he should call to ask about his sister, and when he called it was natural he should sit down for a few minutes.

Somehow, he very soon knew exactly the times when father had to be at the station, and mother was busy with his sister, and I was at work in the kitchen ; and those were the times he chose for coming. I didn't mean to make any secret of his calls, but still I am afraid I did not speak out so plain as I ought.

Things went on so for ten days at least, and I

saw little of Rupert. He seemed to shrink into
himself, and to keep away from me. I suppose
my words that day had cut deep, and he couldn't
forget them.

I don't think he and Mr. Russell met often,
though they slept under one roof. Each did his
best to avoid the other.

As the days went on, I thought less and less of
Rupert, and my mind was more and more given to
this new friend. Ought I to call him "friend?"

We had little chats together, and I began to feel
how well I knew him. I could not help feeling,
too, how much he liked me. His face would light
up at the sight of mine. I wondered often how I
could ever have thought that I might some day
marry Rupert. Poor dull Rupert! so different
from this handsome Mr. Russell, with his nice
manners!

Nearly a fortnight had gone by, and Miss Russell
was doing as well as possible, when all at once she
had a relapse.

The afternoon was hot and sunny, and she
seemed better than any day yet. Mother sent me
to sit with Miss Russell, and took the kitchen
work herself. I would rather have been in the
kitchen, for Mr. Russell was pretty sure to look
in; but mother was determined, and I had to do
as I was bid.

At first I felt cross; only it was not possible
to be cross long with Miss Russell—she was so
gentle always. Somehow she got to talking about

her own young days, and the parents she had lost, and the struggle life had been. She must have worked hard, very hard, to support her brother and herself, and to have him educated for a schoolmaster.

"But hard work doesn't seem so hard for those one loves," she said. "I have always loved Walter dearly—almost as a mother loves, I think. He is more like my child than my brother."

"And he is so fond of you," I said.

"Yes,—I suppose so," she said slowly. "I am not sure that I look much for the return love. It is enough for me to be needful to him. Still, —yes, he *is* fond of me."

"I am sure he is! He was dreadfully unhappy about you when you were ill," I said.

She smiled, and said—"Poor Walter! always up and down."

"I think it would have broken his heart if you had not got better," I said.

"O no!" and a curious look came into her face. "No fear of that. I love my Walter dearly— more dearly than you can tell. I love him as one loves only where one has brought up and sheltered and toiled for another through years. But love does not blind me to his faults. Perhaps I see them the more clearly just because my love is so strong."

I wondered what she meant; and feeling her eyes upon me, my colour went up.

"He has his faults," she said, "and his weaknesses. Don't you think so, Kitty?"

"Yes, of course. Everybody has faults," I answered. "I shouldn't think he has so many as some people."

"Quite as many." And Miss Russell sighed. "It was a difficult thing for me," says she, "very difficult, left alone with him, and I—his sister— only a girl. To be sure, I was many years older; still, I did find it hard to control him properly. I am afraid I didn't. I let him have too much of his own way,—a great deal too much. One sees the ill effects now: he can't understand being denied anything. Yes, that is true, though he is a man, and a clever man, and good at managing boys, —at least, pretty good. He can never understand being opposed. It's a bad look-out for his future wife, whoever she may be. I little thought, when I spoilt the boy, that I was so cruel to other people as well as to him."

I kept silence, sure that Miss Russell must be wrong. It was strange that she should judge her brother harshly—she, of all people, so gentle as she seemed. And why should she say all this to me? Why——? But a thought came in reply which turned me hot all over. Did she think, or know, that he wanted to have me for a wife? Was that it? I couldn't look up or meet her eyes.

She laid her cool hand against my cheeks, which were burning.

"Little Kitty, you are very young," she said. "Don't—don't be in a hurry. Perhaps some day—— "

Then she stopped and thought, and presently she asked—

"What of young Bowman? I hear you and he are great friends."

"He may call himself so," I said, and I could have cried.

"Is that all? I fancied——"

"We know him very well," I said; "and he likes us. So, I suppose, we are friends. Only he gets so——"

"So what?" she asked.

"So cross," I said—"and disagreeable. I hate people to be cross and disagreeable."

"You would like to bask in sunshine always, wouldn't you?"

"I like people to be good-tempered, and not silly and jealous," I said.

"Jealousy is always silly, isn't it?" she said; "but when people love very much, with a love not very unselfish, perhaps——"

I made a sort of movement of impatience.

"He is a steady young fellow," she went on; "your mother tells me so. He has right principles and a warm heart. Kitty, don't you think, some day—?"

I only said, "No!" but I meant it from my very heart.

"Poor fellow!" she said. "Well, you are right not to make up your mind quickly to—anything. I did once, and I had reason to be sorry. O it was just the old story, dear. He thought he loved,

and he won my love; and then he grew tired of
me, and went off after somebody else. That so
often happens."

"With some men, I suppose," I whispered.

"Yes, with some men; not with all. I could
fancy that young Bowman would be constant, not
changeable. If he once cared thoroughly for anybody, he would go on caring. Walter is different.
He does not mean to treat anybody with unkind-
ness, of course, but it seems as if he never could
know his own mind."

What did make her say such things of her
brother? I was growing angry.

"I have seen it in him again and again," she
went on; "so I really have almost given up
believing in his devotion to anybody. He is so
easily caught, and he so easily breaks loose. I
wish I could persuade him to go home now. It is
not good for a young man to be staying in a strange
place, with nothing whatever to do."

"Father thinks it wonderful how quiet and
contented Mr. Russell is in such a dull village,"
I said.

"And your mother quotes old Watts about 'idle
hands.' A woman often sees farther than a man,
Kitty. My brother finds amusement of some sort,
or he would not be so willing to stay. The question
is, what sort of amusement? An idle young
fellow has it in his power to work mischief,
unless——"

"I thought you were so fond of him," I said.

And I did feel hurt for Mr. Russell—not there to defend himself.

"Yes—more than fond," she answered. "I love him with more than a sister's love, my dear. It is like a mother's love, I believe, for it can see his faults and look to what is for his good."

That was all that passed, for she had talked more than she ought. I felt rubbed the wrong way by her words. I knew she meant them as a sort of warning to me, and I didn't like it; I didn't want to be warned; I wanted to be let alone. My head was getting more and more full of Mr. Russell, and his soft words were fast winning my foolish little heart. I didn't want to be warned off from him; and I dreaded lest she should say anything to father or mother. She had not done so yet, I knew.

An hour later father happened to ask—"Russell been in to-day?"

"Yes," says mother, who was with us both for a moment, and she spoke drily. "He came to ask after his sister, and I was in the kitchen."

"Ah!" says father.

"I've no notion of him dangling about when you and I aren't there," said she.

"No, no; quite right," said he. "But, all the same, I like him, Kate. He's a nice young fellow, I do believe."

"I don't!" mother said to herself; and she spoke no more. She never would argue with father, and wisely, too. Nobody is convinced by arguing.

Well, it was perhaps an hour later still, and getting dark, when mother called to me. And when I ran in, there was a dreadful sight! The bleeding had come on afresh, almost as much as ever. Miss Russell did look bad.

"Send or go for the doctor, Kitty, and don't lose a moment!" says mother, and I rushed off, only stopping to seize my hat. There was nobody at hand to be sent just then, and I could not wait to find any one.

The doctor was out, but the servant promised to let him know as quick as possible.

CHAPTER IV.

TWICE GOOD-BYE!

MARY RUSSELL was as near as possible gone that night. I'd better stop calling her "Miss Russell:" for mother always spoke to her as "Mary" by that time, and she had told me to do the same, though I wasn't altogether in the way of it yet.

Mother would not let me sit up late, but I was down early next morning. Needful enough I should: for there was everything to do, and mother not able to be five minutes out of the sick-room.

The doctor came in before breakfast, and he seemed better satisfied; but she wasn't to stir nor to speak, and the brother wasn't to be let in. "No, certainly not! keep *him* out!" Mr. Baitson said, speaking quite sharp, when mother asked. I was puzzled to hear him, for Mr. Baitson wasn't given to speaking sharp.

At five o'clock I left my bed, and I worked hard too; so things were well on by the time father had done his breakfast. I had to go upstairs then for a time; and when I came downstairs I wanted a bit of parsley from the garden, and I ran out.

It was a lovely morning; all a blaze of sunshine, and such a blue sky overhead. Every leaf was sprinkled with big drops of dew wherever there was shade; and the birds were singing like wild. It did seem sad that the poor thing indoors should suffer so much. I stood still a moment, thinking of her, with a feeling as if it was selfish of me to enjoy the sweet air as I did. Then I saw the morning express was signalled, and I waited to see it rush thundering past, though there was no need this time for me to wave a red flag of warning.

When the train was gone, I thought I would take one little run to the end of the path on the top of the embankment, just to freshen up myself for the rest of my work. I was so used to a breath of fresh air early, when mother could spare me.

So I ran, not looking ahead; and all at once I found myself close to Mr. Russell.

He was sitting on the bench beside the gate; the same bench where I had found mother's red shawl that other day. He seemed perfectly wretched. I never saw any man look more miserable than he did just then, dropping the corners of his mouth, and hanging his head, as if he'd got no spirit to sit up.

The moment when I caught sight of him was just the moment when he caught sight of me, and that wasn't till I was near.

"Kitty !" says he, and a sort of groan came with the word. He had never called me so before, but

E

I suppose he forgot. "Kitty," he said, "how is my poor Mary?"

"O I think she's a little better," I said. "Not worse, and that is something."

"Mr. Baitson been again?" he asked.

"Not since breakfast," I said.

"Poor Mary!" says Mr. Russell, and he sighed like a furnace.

" I hope she is going to get on now," I said, for I thought he wanted cheering.

Mr. Russell sighed again.

"And I *would* make her come this journey," he said, self-reproachful like. "If I had been content to stay at home as she wanted, she might have been all right now, and as merry as a grig."

Somehow I could not fancy Mary Russell exactly merry. It wasn't her way.

"You could not know beforehand what would happen," I said.

"Well, no, that's true," he said, and he brightened up. "Nobody can know beforehand what'll happen. That's true enough. It's a horrid thought that if she didn't get well—— But after all, I'd got my reasons for coming away, just as much as she'd got her reasons for wanting to be at home. She needn't have been with me if she hadn't wanted. As you say, one can't tell beforehand how things are going to turn out. Kitty, you're a little comfort!" and he looked up at me, sitting on the bench still, while I stood on the path. "May I call you 'Kitty'—sometimes?"

I said, I shouldn't mind if he did. What else was I to say? Easy enough now to know how I ought to have answered, but not easy at the moment.

"Kitty, I wish I could have you for my little comfort always!" says he, fetching another sigh.

My cheeks got as red as fire, and I didn't say a word.

"I've never seen anybody like you," says he softly, looking at me again. "No, never! Kitty, do you know how pretty you are?"

"I mustn't stop. I've got all the work to do," I said, knowing mother wouldn't like this. And yet I did not want to go. His soft words took hold of me. I thought that to be "his little comfort always" would be the best happiness I could have.

"So busy!" says he. "Ah! I should like you to be where you needn't work; able to sit still and amuse yourself, and have folks to wait upon you."

Little goose that I was, I thought this sounded first-rate. As if anybody was ever the happier for being idle! There's different kinds of work, no doubt; and everybody is happiest doing the sort of work for which he's best fitted by nature and training. No; I don't know as I've put that rightly either: for everybody's happiest doing the work which God has set him to do; and if he isn't fit for it by nature, God can shape him into fitness. But to have no work at all to do means nothing but discontent and unhappiness.

"That's what I should like," he said again. "To

have lots of money, and a nice house, and you to sit there in a pretty parlour, with pretty dresses, and plenty of servants, and nothing ever to bother you."

Easy to see he had never kept house. If he had, he wouldn't have talked in the same breath about "plenty of servants" and "nothing to bother." But I didn't see through his words then.

"Well, I may be rich yet one day," he went on. "Who knows? And when I am—you may be sure I'll not forget. Kitty," says he slowly, "supposing some day I was to ask you to cast in your lot with me, when I'm a rich man? Or supposing I didn't wait to be rich?"

It was not an easy question to answer. For mind you, he didn't say, "Will you cast in your lot with me?" but only, "Supposing I was to ask you?" That might mean anything or nothing.

My heart went pit-a-pat, and I hung my head. His next words were not what I looked for.

"Kitty," he said, "you mustn't tell anybody what I said just now. If you do, I shall have to leave by the next train, and never come back. Promise you won't."

And I, like a little goose again, frightened at the thought of driving him away, and never waiting to consider what was due to my father and mother, was so in his power that I said, "No, I won't!"

The moment the words had passed my lips, I knew they were wrong; yet I did not try to take them back.

"That's my own little Kitty!" he said. He

spoke in an undertone, but I heard the words; and I felt as if all the world was changed to me. His own little Kitty! Was I to be that? It wasn't till later that I noticed he hadn't asked if I wanted to be anything of the sort. He seemed to take all that for granted, which no man has ever a right to do with any woman. But at the moment I could only be joyful.

The next instant Mr. Russell was saying in a careless loud voice—

" Yes, I'm going for a stroll, and then I shall call again to see how poor Mary is getting on."

The change of voice gave me a sort of stunned feeling. I couldn't think what he meant, and all that had gone before looked unreal. Then I understood, for Rupert was walking along the path straight toward us.

" Your mother wants you, Kitty," he says in a short gruff voice, as he came up. He always spoke to me now in that voice; and he didn't so much as cast a look at Mr. Russell.

" Indoors ? " I asked.

" Where else ? " Rupert answered.

" Well, you might speak civil when you bring a message," I said, foolishly enough, for where was the use of angering him ?

" Civil ! " burst out Rupert, and something in the tone frightened me, it was so sore and fierce. I just said, " I'm going," and ran straight off, my cheeks burning still, and a strange new happiness beating at my heart.

Not all happiness, though. It could not be all
happiness for a girl to be sought in such a fashion.
For it was as if Mr. Russell was afraid or ashamed
to speak out.

I could not see why he should fear. Father
had taken to him from the first; and if mother
didn't do that, at least she never snubbed him,
which was, I suppose, because of his trouble about
Mary, for mother *could* snub, and no mistake!

But why should he not go to them, and say
plain out that he wanted me? That was the
question.

He had not so much as asked whether I cared
for him! I could have been vexed to remember
this, if only I had cared for him less. He seemed
so sure that he only had to ask me, and I would
jump at it. At least he had only said, "Suppose,"
in a way that mightn't mean anything.

And I was not to tell a word to my father or
mother. That was hard. I had never had a
regular secret from them before; and I was so used
to speaking out. It didn't feel natural to have to
hold my tongue.

But I had promised! I had said I wouldn't
tell! And I had been brought up to think a deal
of keeping my word.

Many a time mother had said to me, "Mind
you, Kitty, a promise is a promise! Don't you
ever make one lightly; and when it is made, don't
you ever break it lightly."

Right enough too. To my mind there's judg-

ment on the breaking of a promise; no matter how
small a one. It's "least said, soonest mended," in
the matter of promises, as well as in most other
things. A promise once given can't be taken back,
without the consent of the person it's given to;
and a broken promise can't be mended.

I can remember once, when I was a little child,
mother was away for the whole day, and she promised to bring me a packet of pink candy. Somebody said to me, "Oh, you mustn't count on that;
she's pretty sure to forget!" And I stamped my
foot, and said, "Mother won't forget! Mother
always keeps her promise!"

Well, and I was in the right. She kept her
promise, and brought the candy. But she did
forget for a while; for there was an accident, which
upset her, and drove it out of her head. On the
way home she recollected. Some would have said,
"Oh, it's too late now! It can't be helped, and
Kitty must wait!" But mother wasn't that sort.
She went near a mile back to the only shop where
the pink candy could be got; and we all wondered
what was making her so late.

If she hadn't! Well, of course, she could have
said she had forgot, and she was sorry.

You don't think, though, do you, that I should
ever have felt so certain sure again, when she promised? I should always have thought, she might
forget!

Ah! mother was a rare one. There's not many
like her. She wasn't overmuch given to promises

at any time; but once she did promise, she'd do it.

And I had promised Mr. Russell not to tell. I had promised lightly—that's to say, without weighing it first. Was I to break the promise lightly?

Something whispered to me, as I went back, dropping into a slow walk—something whispered, "Tell out plain to Mr. Russell that the promise was wrong, and that you can't keep it."

But I did not like the idea. I knew he would be so vexed, and I could not bear to vex him. I feared it might drive him away from me for always. The wish to please him stood out first, not the wish to do what was right.

I began to have a feeling that all my happiness was bound up in him. For days past I had let myself think a deal too much about Mr. Russell; and now the words he had spoken had taken me altogether captive. Rupert was nothing to me any more. I was ready to leave father, mother, home, everything—for him.

It is natural for a girl to feel so; natural and not wrong, when other things are right. If Mr. Russell had been a man of the right stamp, coming openly and honestly to seek me, with my parents' consent, there was no reason why I shouldn't be willing.

Only, I didn't know him at all to be a man of the right stamp; and he had not said a word to my father or mother. He had got me to promise not to tell them either. That was wrong to begin

with. And if the first step into a path is wrong,
then each step after which takes one along the path
is only a going more astray.

Mother saw me pass the window, and she came
into the kitchen. I felt her eyes on my face, and
I could not look up to meet them.

" Where have you been ? " asked she.

" In the garden, mother," I said, hanging my head,
and wishing my cheeks didn't burn so.

" That's nothing to be ashamed of, is it ? " says
she. " What took you into the garden ? "

" I—wanted some parsley," I said. For a moment
I couldn't recollect what had taken me first.

" Did the parsley keep you all this time ? " says
she, as quiet as anything.

" No, mother," I said; " it wasn't only the parsley.
It was—I went along the path. And Mr. Russell
was there. He came to ask ——"

" To ask about Mary, I suppose ? " says mother,
in her dry-like tone. " Yes; but he heard about
her just an hour ago, Kitty. He's in a great hurry
to hear again."

" She's so ill," I said.

" Yes, that's true. She's been worse," mother
said.

" And he seemed—he seemed—so unhappy," I
went on. " I just stayed a minute—to—to comfort—— " And then the thought of the way he
had used that word, calling me " a little comfort,"
rushed up, and my cheeks burnt redder than ever.

" To comfort him ! " says she. " Yes, that's very

pretty. But you're a young woman now, Kitty, and he is a young man. So next time you find him unhappy, you had best come straight and tell me, and I'll do the comforting."

Mother meant it for a rebuke, I knew, though she didn't speak angrily; for it never was her way to show anger.

But she did not suspect how things really were. That was plain enough. If she had had the least suspicion, she would not have taken it so quiet. She was afraid of me getting to like Mr. Russell overmuch; yet all the same she trusted me. It went to my heart with a stab that mother should trust me so, when I wasn't worthy of it. I longed to speak out plain and tell her everything; yet I couldn't bear to do what would vex Mr. Russell. So I clung to my secret, though it made me miserable.

I had told her the truth, but not the whole truth, and mother had a right to know the whole. My promise to Mr. Russell could not undo her rights nor father's rights over me, a mere girl of seventeen. The promise was wrong; and whether I kept it or whether I broke it, either way I should be doing wrong. That's the sort of muddle that hasty speech gets one into. Once plunge into a quagmire, and whichever way you get out there's sure to be some of the mire sticking to you.

The question for me was—Which of the two ways would be the *most* wrong, since neither could be altogether right? But I didn't care to look

that question in the face. I didn't want to find
that I ought not to keep my promise. I liked to
feel that I was bound to silence, even while it
grieved me not to be open with mother.

Mary Russell began to get better much faster
from this second attack than from the first. Still,
for a few days, mother was a deal taken up with
her; and I'm ashamed to say how often I saw Mr.
Russell.

He was always meeting me somehow—out of
doors or in the garden, or else calling to ask after
his sister just when he knew he might catch a
word with me alone. I didn't see then that this
was deceit, or that I was helping forward the
deceit; at least, I didn't let myself think that I
saw it so.

I got so to feed upon his looks and words, so to
crave for another and another glimpse, that there
seemed to be no room for anything else in my
head. Work was hurried over or left undone
many a time those days. Mother said nothing
in haste; she only watched and waited. I don't
think she had an idea how far things went; but
she was afraid her Kitty's silly little heart was
being caught in a net, and she was on the look-out
to prevent it.

Ah, but she could not, for I was not open and
true with her; and no mother's love, or any other
love, can guard against the evil results of deceit.

When Mr. Russell and I were alone he would
call me again "his own little Kitty," and the words

made my heart spring with joy—only it was a
secret trembling joy, which feared to be found out.
But he took care not to call me "Kitty" before
anybody.

Sometimes I was on the very edge of asking him
to let me tell mother, and yet again I was afraid.
For all this while he had never once exactly put
the question—Would I promise to marry him ?
He only seemed perfectly sure that if he did put
it I should say, "Yes."

That wasn't a state of things father nor mother
would have allowed.

"Kitty," he said one day, all of a sudden, "I've
got to go to-morrow."

Mother had sent me to a shop for some thread,
and Mr. Russell came upon me just outside the
station, in the little lane that ran round the back of
our garden.   I suppose he must have been expecting me there.   Nobody else was in sight.   We
stood under the high hedge, on a patch of grass, and
I can remember now the feel of the grass under
my feet, and the sunset light that came through
the hedge opposite, and how handsome Mr. Russell
looked—at least, I thought so then ; but, you know,
girls' tastes do change as they get to womanhood,
and it isn't only black hair and eyes and an air
of being somebody that makes good looks—more
especial if it's a case of being nobody.

"Must you ? " was all I said, and I turned queer
all over, as if I was ready to drop.

"Yes; it's a 'must,'" says he. "I shall have to be at work again in a few days, and there's a lot of things to do first. I've been here too long as it is."

"But you couldn't help it, with Mary so ill," I said.

He gave a sort of little laugh.

"Well—yes," says he. "But Mary's been getting on all right some days past. You don't think it's that has kept me, do you? eh, Kitty?" says he. "Can't you guess what has been the real tie? Not good old Mary, but somebody younger and prettier and sweeter?"

Yes, I guessed what he meant, of course. I couldn't do otherwise, and the colour came back to my face.

"It is very hard to say good-bye to that somebody, I can tell you," said he. "But never mind. You'll soon see me again."

"How soon?" I asked, with such a heart-sinking: for it seemed as if all the world was going when he went.

"Oh, soon," he said. "As soon as ever I can get away. Those little school brats take up a lot of time, you know. But I shouldn't wonder if I had to come and fetch Mary soon."

"Will it be next week?" I tried to say.

"Next week! Dear, no! not so soon as that. Why, the doctor says it won't be safe for Mary to go by train for another month; and I mightn't be able to get away just then, you know. But I'll come, never you fear! Why, Kitty, you dear little pretty silly thing," says he, "I'm not worth crying for!"

It was true, but did he mean it? I've often thought of his face since, as it was that moment, and wondered if the look meant real pity or was only just put on.

"I shan't know how to get on without you," I whispered.

"Well, but it won't be for long. I'll be sure to come again," says he. Then he added, "Mind you keep my secret, Kitty!"

"Mayn't I just tell mother?" I begged.

"Tell your mother!" he said; and I couldn't understand his face. "Tell her what?" says he.

I was struck dumb. For what had I to tell? That he wished me to be his wife? But he had never asked me if I would, never once outright! That he called me "his little Kitty?" But he had no right to call me so.

"No, it won't do yet," said he. "I can't let you speak out yet, Kitty. You don't understand why, of course; but it won't do. I'm not in a position to have it known yet, and till I am, you mustn't let it be thought that we———" He bungled there, and didn't finish his sentence. "I should only be told I wasn't to see you again, and you wouldn't like that, eh? No, we've got to wait a while."

"But if it isn't right—if I ought to tell?" I got out feebly. You see, I'd given in so long, it was doubly hard to make a stand then.

He laughed at this.

"Wrong!" says he. "Why, you dear little goose, what's right or wrong to do with it? And, in point of fact, there's nothing to tell," says he. "We've not settled anything; only you're a dear little charming Kitty, and—well, you like me, don't you?"

"How do you know I like you?" I asked.

"That's not so hard to see," said he, laughing again. "I mightn't have been so sure at first, if I hadn't had a word from a friend of yours; but I can't feel any manner of doubt now."

I knew he meant Mrs. Hammond: yet I could not be angry just then, with him going away next day.

"And I like you too, of course," he went on. "So it is give and take, isn't it? All fair and square, you know. You're the prettiest and sweetest girl I've ever seen in all my life. That's saying a good deal, isn't it? And some day—— Well, you've got to go indoors now, I suppose, and you can tell Mary I shan't be able to see her in the morning, because I must be off by the early train. I've seen her this afternoon, and she knows I'm going."

The sharp change of voice took me all aback, as when there had been the same once before; and the cause was the same too; for once again Rupert stood staring hard at us, with a strange look, as if his mouth was made of iron.

I heard a sort of mutter from Mr. Russell, which

sounded like—"Meddlesome chap!" Rupert said nothing. He only stood stock-still, and stared.

"Well, it's getting late, and I must be gone. Good-bye, Kitty," said Mr. Russell.

He must have been flurried by Rupert's sudden coming, to call me "Kitty" before another. I saw it was a forget, by his start; but the word once said couldn't be unsaid, and I suppose he thought he'd better carry it off well, so he gave a little laugh, and repeated, "Good-bye, Kitty!" in a tone as if he'd been speaking to a child.

Then he was gone; and Rupert and I were left together. I would have run away, but I did not.

"You've been crying," Rupert said, very short.

"It's not your business if I have," I said.

"About that worthless chap, I suppose? And he daring to call you 'Kitty!'" Rupert looked as if he was ready to foam at the mouth, and yet it was in a sort of dead-quiet way, not like a man in a regular passion.

"You call me 'Kitty,'" I said, "and I'd rather you wouldn't."

"Kitty, this can't go on," says he in a hoarse voice.

"No. I would rather you should leave off calling me 'Kitty,'" I said, not knowing what he meant by "this." "I'm not a child now," I said, "and I don't like the way you behave."

"Behave!" Rupert burst out, and then he pulled himself in, and spoke quiet again: "What will your mother say, Kitty?"

"Say to what?" I asked.

"When I tell her I found you two here! Sort of tender leave-taking, wasn't it?"

I could not guess how much he had seen or heard, and I would not stoop to ask him not to speak: so I did not say a word.

"Kitty, this can't go on!" says he again.

"What can't? I don't know what you mean, and I don't care!" I said, in a pet with him, because I was so unhappy. "You are cruel to me, Rupert; and I hate you when you plague me like this."

"You—hate—me!" Rupert said the words slowly. The light fell full on his face—only a rough plain boyish face; but such a look of sorrow and love came into it that moment as I had never seen before, and it seemed to change the whole face. He put out both his hands towards me for a moment, with a sort of longing; but I don't think he knew he did that. Then he folded his arms tight, and the softness went out of his eyes, and his mouth grew hard and cold.

"No, it can't go on," he said. "I've borne as much as I could; and I can't bear more. I can't be untrue, and I can't betray you! That's where it is. You see, Kitty, I *can't* hate you back, and I can't make myself not care. There's nothing for me but to go right away. You needn't tell my mother it was you who drove me to it! She'll understand."

"Rupert, what nonsense you are talking!" I said,

F

only half taking in what he said, for my mind
was with Mr. Russell. "What nonsense! How
can you say such foolish things? I don't know
what you mean by 'going away.' It is nonsense.
I don't want to vex you, if only you wouldn't
behave so unbearably. I can't be spied and
meddled with, and I can't pretend to like you
more than I do."

"No, there's no sort of pretence about it," says
Rupert. "None at all. Folks don't 'pretend' to
hate; and you 'hate' me. I could stand anything
short of that, Kitty. Except seeing you throw yourself away on an empty-headed puppy, who'll make
your life a burden to you. So I'm off; it don't
matter where! and this is another good-bye."

He went away slowly with his shuffling walk, not
straight and quick like Mr. Russell. I noticed
that, and at first I felt almost like laughing. For
I little thought how deep my words had cut.
There's many a word that goes in like a knife, and
leaves a wound which doesn't heal for years.
But I didn't see that, or believe what he said.
Go away! It was so ridiculous. He had nowhere
to go, and there was his work at the station, and
his mother and sister couldn't do without him.

I half laughed, though my heart was so sore
for Mr. Russell that tears lay nearer than laughter.
Then I thought of the strange look that had come
to Rupert's face, and I called out "Rupert!" but
had no answer. "Rupert!" I cried again. It was
too late. He had gone out of hearing. And, after

all, what matter ? I could tell him in the morning
that I had only been cross, and that I had not
really meant anything so bad as " hating ; " only
he must leave off meddling and saying hard words
to me.

I went back into the house, for I knew mother
would be expecting me. She gave a look up, and
said—

" What's the matter ? "

" I'm—tired," I said. My feet seemed to have
turned to lead, and I felt as if I would do anything to have a good cry.

" Sit down and rest," says she. " You've gone
as white as a sheet."

But I didn't dare sit down and think, for I
couldn't have kept up then. The thought of
Rupert was fading away like smoke. I could
only feel that Mr. Russell was gone, and that
everything was different.

" I must get in help," mother said. " You've
done too much lately."

" O no," I said.

" Yes. Mary will be here another month : Mr.
Baitson says so ; and I'm glad enough to keep her ;
but I can't have you knocked up."

After a minute, mother said—

" Mr. Russell is going."

I didn't say a word.

" He's been in to bid Mary good-bye. It's
rather sudden. I'm not sorry for my part," mother
said.

I stood leaning against the dresser, and felt as if I must choke. Mother gave me another look. Then she came close, and put her arms round me; and I clung to her, and cried—oh, how I did cry! Mother just petted and soothed, and didn't ask a single question; only presently she talked of other things, and tried to lead my thoughts away from him.

For, you see, she hadn't a notion of anything between us two. She only thought her Kitty's silly heart was touched. She trusted me so, she could not fancy anything *said* which I would not tell her. And she had no notion of making matters worse by a lot of talk about Mr. Russell.

CHAPTER V.

RUPERT.

"WHAT'S become of Rupert?" father said at breakfast next day.

We always breakfasted at half-past seven, partly because father had to be up so early, and partly because mother liked it. Rupert ought to have been in the ticket-office half-an-hour before, in time for the first passenger-train that stopped at Claxton. Plenty of luggage-trains went by in the night, but happily for father and the men, there wasn't much shunting of them at our station, like at the next station. They had to work there through a good part of the night.

"Hasn't he come as usual?" mother asked, in answer to father's question. Rupert was so regular, it seemed astonishing he should fail.

"Not a sign of him. If it was anybody else, I'd say he was lazy; but Rupert's not given to laziness. I'm afraid he can't be well," father went on. "We shall hear presently."

Just at the moment I did not remember what Rupert had said to me the evening before. It would be thought more natural for me to remember at-once, but I didn't.   My head was so full of the thought of Mr. Russell.

"Anybody come or go?" mother asked.   It was the very question I wanted to put, only I had not courage.

"Russell has left.   That's all," father said.

Then he was really gone!   A sick feeling came over me, and I couldn't eat my breakfast.   I knew mother saw, and I knew she wouldn't say a word : she'd always such a notion of the harm done by too many words.   But father happened to look my way.

"Why—Kitty!" says he.   "The child's not well."

"She has had too much to do lately," said mother.   "Kitty's not overstrong."

"Why, she's as white ——" father said.   "Come here, Kitty, and let's see what's wrong."

I came as I was bidden, and he took hold of me, looking hard.   I couldn't stand that.   The next moment I was clinging to him, with my face down on his shoulder.

Maybe mother made him some sort of sign.   I shouldn't wonder if she did; for he cuddled me in his arms as if I'd been a small child again, and whispered—"Poor little kittenkins!" once or twice, which was my old nursery name.   But he didn't ask any more questions.

"She's been a good girl to help so steady all through Mary's illness," mother said presently.   "I wish now I'd had a girl in to help; and I might have done it, but I thought I'd lay by what the Russells paid us.   Maybe I've been penny wise and pound foolish, for once. But I did think, too, the work was good for Kitty."

"So it is! so it was!" says father. "Good for everybody. And a good thing to lay by a few shillings too! But it isn't worth while to make our Kitty ill. That 'ud cost a lot more shillings than we could have laid by. Eh, Kitty? Come, cheer up!" says he. "We'll see what we can do to make you right again."

How good they were to me, both father and mother!—and I deceiving them all the while!

"Now I must go and see if Rupert has turned up," says father. "Kitty must get a run on the common, eh?"

And all at once it darted into my head about Rupert the evening before, and how he had said good-bye. I started up in a moment.

"O father! Oh, see about Rupert!" I cried, hardly able to speak yet, but scared at the thought that had come to me.

"To be sure I will," says he. "You wouldn't like Rupert to be ill, eh?"

"I hope he is—I hope it is that—I hope it isn't anything worse," I cried, scarce knowing what I said; and father did stare, but I went on, pretty near out of breath with fright—

"Oh, do make haste and see."

"To be sure I will," says father again. "Why, Kitty, what's come over you to-day?"

That very moment the kitchen door was pushed open, and Mrs. Bowman stood there.

She was a puny sad-faced woman at the best of times, one of those folks who take life hard, and never get any pleasure out of it; but I'd never seen her look so haggard before.

"Where's—Rupert?" she said, and she fixed her eyes on father.

"That's the very question I've been wanting to ask you," father said.

"Sit down, Mrs. Bowman," says mother. "Sit down and tell us what's gone wrong."

Mrs. Bowman dropped into a chair, close to where she was standing.

"He came in late last night," she said. "And he wouldn't say where he'd been. And he wouldn't take his supper. And he looked so strange. And this morning he never came to breakfast. And his door was locked. And he didn't answer. And when we got in he wasn't there. And his bed wasn't slept in. And a lot of his things are gone!"

"Poor dear!" mother says, pitying-like, as the "And" got to be a gasp, and then a sob. "I shouldn't have thought it of Rupert."

"But you don't think he's—gone!" father said.

"Yes, I do think it," Mrs. Bowman cried, in a weak, broken sort of voice. "I do think it, and I'm sure of it! Kitty knows why! If you ask Kitty she can tell. She's driven him off, and that's what she's done."

"Kitty!" father said, looking at me.

Then he walked up to Mrs. Bowman.

"Come, come, that's nonsense, you know," says he. "Kitty and Rupert are good enough friends, and always have been ; but Kitty's not bound to favour him special, Mrs. Bowman. You can't say she is. And what's more, she's a deal too young for that sort of nonsense; if it's that you mean. Kitty's a child still, and Rupert's another. If he's got into a huff about Kitty, so much the worse for him ; but I don't see that Kitty's to blame. However, I hope the lad's not so silly. I've got to go to the station now, and you'd best come along with me. I shouldn't wonder if we find Rupert there, all right. It's been a freak, going off early this morning—at least I hope so ; and he'll be back soon, if he isn't back yet. Come along ! If he's not at the station, I'll go home with you, and we'll think what to do."

Father went off, walking sharp, and Mrs. Bowman trailed after him in a weak way, as if she wasn't sure whether she'd go or stay. Then mother said—

"What does it mean, Kitty ? "

"Rupert has been so—tiresome, lately."

"Tiresome what way ? " says she.

"Oh, just getting cross," I said.

"What about ? " says she.

"He'd got a notion," I said.

"Yes—a notion ? " says she, waiting as quiet as anything, and I knew she didn't mean to let me off.

"He wanted—wanted me—to—marry him," I said, crying anew. "And I—couldn't."

"How do you know he wanted that?" said she.

"He said it one day. And I ran away and left him, mother."

"Not a bad plan," says she. "I wish a few more girls would run away from a few more lads. There'd be a lot of trouble spared. Well, how long ago was it?"

I had to think a moment, before I could remember that it was just before the express train having to be stopped.

"Rupert was wrong to speak to you," mother said. "He ought to have come first to father and me."

But I thought of Mr. Russell, and I didn't say "Yes."

"He was so vexed," I said. "And he's been angry and disagreeable since. And yesterday evening he told me—told me—he meant to go away. I didn't believe him. I thought it was all nonsense."

"When did he tell you?"

"Out-of-doors," I said.

"When, Kitty?" says she again.

"When I was coming back from the shop," I said, wishing mother wouldn't put so many questions.

"Ah—was it Rupert who kept you so long?" says mother, looking straight at me, and I felt myself get scarlet.

"I saw Rupert—then," I said. "And—I met Mr. Russell too—and he told me he was going—and said—good-bye."

It was hard to get that word out; but I felt
sure mother had an idea of Mr. Russell, and I
knew if I didn't tell she'd ask.

"Ah——!" says she again.

"Rupert needn't have been so cross and jealous,"
I went on.

"Jealous, was he?"

"He can't bear me to speak to—anybody," I
whispered, wishing I hadn't let that word slip.

"He was jealous of Mr. Russell, you mean?"
said mother.

I think I said "Yes," quite low.

Then another question came, which I had been
dreading all along—

"Kitty, did Mr. Russell say anything of that
sort to you too?"

I didn't know what to say, for I dared not tell
a lie.

"Did *he* ever ask you to marry him?" mother
said; and I knew she was drawing a long breath
up and up, as if she felt a weight somewhere.

"No, mother," I said, for he had not.

"No! But he has said soft words, maybe. Soft
words don't cost much, Kitty, nor they don't always
mean much."

I couldn't speak. Mother came close, and I
held her tight, and she sighed again, though she
wasn't given to sighing commonly.

"Well, it can't be helped now," she said. "I
might have had more sense at my time of life. I
do wish I'd been sharper. Kitty, if you're a wise

girl you won't let yourself spend time thinking
about Mr. Russell's soft speeches, nor Rupert's
hard ones.   I don't doubt Rupert's gone off in a
temper, and I shouldn't wonder if he didn't come
back for some days—a week or more, maybe.
That's bad for his mother!   You'll get the credit
of his going, and you'd best take it quiet.   Least
said 'll be soonest mended in the end."

If I had but thought of that the evening before,
and not spoken the hasty words which drove
Rupert away !   Poor foolish boy !

For he was gone.   Father came soon and told
us so.   He wasn't at the station nor anywhere in
the village.   Nobody had seen him.

He didn't come back in a week either !   Mother
was wrong there !

It was a terrible blow for Mrs. Bowman and
Mabel.   Mabel could do fine needlework, and Mrs.
Bowman was used to go out for a day's work ; but
now they would have to keep themselves altogether,
Rupert's wages being gone.

He had done very wrongly ; everybody said
that.   But people blamed me too ; and I knew it,
for Mrs. Hammond told me so.   And if they had
known all, they would have blamed me more.
Wasn't it hard enough that I couldn't return
Rupert's honest love ?   What call had I to go and
say harsh things to him as well, when his heart
was sore already ?   Ah, folks called me humble
and gentle, because I had a soft manner ; but they
didn't know me in those days.   No, not even my

mother knew me fully, and least of all did I know myself.

Another lad came as ticket-collector in Rupert's place; at first, only to fill up the gap for a while, since father and everybody hoped Rupert wouldn't be gone long. But time went on, and he did not return, so at last the post was lost to him.

I could hardly bear to meet Mrs. Bowman or Mabel, they looked so reproachful at me; yet they couldn't really tell what had passed. They only guessed that he had been jealous of Mr. Russell, and vexed not to be liked most.

It came out that Mrs. Hammond had spread all over the village about my saying that I liked Mr. Russell best; and the story was told in a way that made a great deal more of my words than the reality. That's common enough.

When the tale reached mother's ears, it fairly upset her. She did so hate gossip. She had not said a sharp word to me before, since Mr. Russell went; but she did then. She wanted to know all about the truth of the matter; so I told her how Rupert had bothered, and how I had answered him, saying more than I meant, and how Mrs. Hammond had happened to hear, and how she had promised not to repeat, and hadn't kept her word.

"Yes, that is the way," mother said, seeming terribly vexed. "If nobody would ever say what oughtn't to be overheard, there would be a lot less harm done." And then she repeated—"Mrs. Hammond's word! And you expected anything from her promise! That's the sort of woman you can be fond of, is it?"

I was too down-hearted to make much of an answer, or to defend myself, if any defending was needed. After all, mother was a deal more angry for me than with me. She couldn't stand the thought of her Kitty's name being bandied about in such a way among the villagers.

Mary Russell was up and dressed for almost the first time, and able to sit in the garden. She heard mother speaking, and presently she beckoned to me to come and sit by her with my work, while mother was busy indoors.

I didn't mind going, though everything felt so flat and dull those days, with Mr. Russell gone, that I could not care much about anything. However, I took up my work, and dragged myself across to where Mary sat, smiling at the flowers.

"Come, Kitty," says she; and when I was by her, she asked—"Has something gone wrong?"

"It doesn't matter," I said, getting red, for I did not want to explain.

"I think it does," said she, "if it makes Kitty look so unhappy. Come, put down the work, and tell me all about it."

"I can't!" I said, beginning to sew fast.

"I think you can," said she, and she spoke quiet, but in a determined sort of voice that I hadn't heard in her before. "Kitty, tell me! Was it something about my brother?"

I couldn't look up in her face, and I wouldn't say "Yes."

"I think I know part already, and I want to know the rest," she said. "Don't think me meddlesome, for I have a reason."

And she took hold of both my hands, so I couldn't work.

"Look up in my face and tell me," she said. "Is it something about Walter—and Mrs. Hammond—and Rupert—and yourself?"

"It's all nonsense; only Mrs. Hammond's talk," I said, half crying. "It wasn't anything, really. Only Rupert got cross one day and he called Mr. Russell a puppy. He often did that. And he wanted me to promise never to like Mr. Russell better than him. And I told Rupert he was rude, and I said I did like Mr. Russell the best. And Mrs. Hammond heard me, and laughed about it. And I made her promise not to tell, because— because it sounded silly. And she has told."

"Yes; it sounds very silly," Mary said. "But was that all, Kitty? Are you sure? The story has grown."

"Yes, I am sure that was all," I answered. "It couldn't be more. Why, that was the day you came, and I didn't even know Mr. Russell then. I was only cross with Rupert, and wanted to tease him, so I said the first words that came into my head.

"Mrs. Hammond forgot to mention the date," Mary said gravely. "There's a wonderful difference

made by *when* a thing is said. And she didn't put
it exactly in that way, either. She told Walter
that Kitty Phrynne cared more for him than for
anybody, and made no secret of wanting to
marry him."

" O no ! She couldn't say that ! " I cried,
dreadfully ashamed.

" She did, Kitty."

" But—how——? " I tried to ask.

" Walter told me himself—not till yesterday. I
wish I had known sooner."

I turned my head away. Walter had told her !
But in what way had he told ?

Mary seemed to see the question which I could
not ask.

" He laughed a little about it," she said, in a
low voice. " We agreed how absurd it was of Mrs.
Hammond to invent such a story ; for of course it
could not be true. But, Kitty——"

She stopped again, and my heart went down,
down.

" Kitty, I never can be sure if Walter means
or does not mean exactly what he says, or whether
he tells me the whole. I don't know whether you
have found out yet that he does sometimes—that
he is not perfectly straightforward. At first I
understood that he had only just heard this bit
of foolish talk, and then he let slip that he had
known it from the first. I can't help being afraid
that he may, perhaps, in some way have acted
upon it—may have treated you as if ——"

I think she hardly knew what to say, and what
not to say, for she stopped again. She wanted to
find out more, yet she did not want to put into
my head any fancies not there already. I kept my
face turned away, and would not speak.

"Kitty, did he?" she whispered.

Then I looked round suddenly.

"He has always been kind," I said. "Kinder
than Rupert. I think it is a shame of Mrs. Hammond to say such things. I shall never like Mrs.
Hammond again."

"No, you will hardly trust her," Mary said. But
I fancy she had expected something different from
me. She sat still, looking thoughtful, even sad;
and I made an excuse about wanting cotton, and
so got away. I felt so wretched, I could bear
no more.

Yet all this did not shake my belief in Mr.
Russell. If he meant to keep it a secret about
what he and I felt for each other, or what I
thought we felt, he was likely to try to put his
sister off the scent. No doubt he found that Mrs.
Hammond's gossip was getting to be known, and
so he told Mary himself to be beforehand. I
did wonder whether it was that story coming out
which helped to settle him so sudden to leave the
place.

Mary had not done with the matter yet. When
she was in bed, I always slipped in to say a last
good-night, and she liked it. Often she was sleepy,
and said only a word. But that evening she was

G

wide awake, and she took my face between her hands, and looked at it.

"Kitty, you are getting pale," she told me.

"O no," I answered.

"Saying no doesn't alter things," she said.   "Are you poorly?"

"No," I said.

"Poor little Kitty!" she whispered, and she kissed my cheek.

"I'm only come to—say good-night," I said.

"Yes, I know," said she; yet she wouldn't let go. She pulled me down till I lay beside her, with my face against hers, and then she asked—"Kitty, do you ever pray?"

"Yes," I said, "every morning and evening."

"You say your prayers, don't you?" said she. "But is it real praying?"

"I—don't know," I whispered.

"Because there is no such comfort in anything else," she said. "When one is troubled or puzzled, there's nothing like going straight to God, and telling Him all about it. Not only telling, but putting the whole thing into His hands, and asking Him to arrange everything. Do you remember how the disciples went and 'told Jesus' directly they heard of St. John the Baptist's death?"

"Yes," I said faintly.

"And we can do the same about everything—we ought to do the same," she went on. "He is always near—always kind and ready to help. He always answers if we really call upon Him."

I only said " Yes." The words didn't come home to me particularly then, though perhaps they did later.

" I think you are troubled now about something, and puzzled too," said she.

" Oh, I don't know," I said.

" You see, I know so well what that is," she said : " I have been so often puzzled and troubled. It couldn't be otherwise, having to stand alone early, as I have had to do. Sometimes it has been about money matters ; sometimes about somebody else's wrong-doing ; sometimes about my own wrong-doing ; or, perhaps, just not knowing what to do, not being sure which step was right or wrong. And you know, Kitty, one may always come to God, with every wrong, and ask Him to set it right or to help one through. Always ! always !" she repeated very earnestly. " If we can't see our way, He will show it to us. And if we don't know what we ought to do, He will make it clear. We only have to be willing, and to wait for the showing."

But did I want to have it made clear ? That was the question. I wanted to have my own way. I wanted to keep Mr. Russell's secret. I wanted to feel myself bound by the promise I had spoken. I did not want to be shown God's will, unless it were my own will too. So how could I honestly pray for God to guide me to what was right, if I wasn't willing to do what was right when I saw it ?

Mary said no more, and let me go, which was wiser than if she had kept on talking at me.

People commonly don't know when to stop, and they'll spoil the best advice by nagging on too long at it; but that wasn't Mary's way. She had said what was needful, and she said no more. And her words didn't fall to the ground, though at the moment they didn't seem to weigh with me.

I wonder if any words ever do really "fall to the ground." There's a deal of power for good or evil in a word. And there's no measuring the effect of any word. Like a stone thrown into a pond, it sends circle after circle outward, even when it has disappeared itself, and the water over it is smooth.

Once speak a word, and you can't stop circles. They'll go on and on, till they're done. That's the meaning of "least said, soonest mended." And it's true even of good advice, as well as of other sorts of talk. Piling on words don't do good in the end.

I thought a lot of what Mary had said; but I always came round to the same point. I didn't *want* to be freed from my promise.

It was curious how many things happened together that year. Sometimes it does seem so in life; ever so many uncommon events near after one another, and then a long spell with nothing particular.

There was Rupert's asking me to marry him; and the narrow escape of a bad collision; and the Earl giving me his watch; and my silly little head being turned. Then there was Mary Russell's illness; and her brother always about; till my silly little heart was turned too. And then Mr. Russell bidding good-bye, and Rupert running away.

It didn't seem likely anything more would happen out of the common yet awhile. But one never can tell. That's the strangest part of life. However steady the days seem to go on, one never can be sure of a single day ahead.

No, I don't know either that that is the strangest. There's something stranger yet in the way we manage to go slipping and sliding along, never able to see if a precipice don't lie just ahead, and yet not troubling ourselves, but expecting things to keep on always the same. At least, that's how it is with some people. Some are over-anxious, and some don't think enough. It's right to trust God for our future; but it isn't right to be reckless and indifferent.

Something lay ahead that summer, which mother and I little dreamed of. If we had—but, after all, isn't it a mercy that we don't see what's coming? Only I do think we should be wiser to live more as if things *might* come, so that we shouldn't need to be saying afterward with a heart-ache—" Ah ! if only I'd guessed, how different I'd have behaved to him or her ! "

But I've got more to tell first, before coming to that sorrow.

About a month after the evening when Mr.

Russell and I said good-bye to one another in the lane, Mary Russell left us. She was ever so much better by that time, and Mr. Baitson was quite willing she should travel. He'd have given leave a week sooner, I believe, only mother wouldn't let Mary go.

For days before she went, I was all in a quake and stir, thinking how Mr. Russell would run over to Claxton to fetch her. He wouldn't surely let her travel alone, after such an illness.

But nobody seemed to think of such a thing, and not a word was spoken about it. I wanted to ask Mary if he didn't mean to come, and I couldn't, for the words stuck in my throat. It wasn't till the last evening before she left, when she and I went for a turn in the garden, after dusk fell, and I knew she couldn't see my face, that I managed to say—

"Is Mr. Russell coming to take you home, Mary?"

I wanted to speak careless-like, and as if it was a thing I didn't mind about either way; but I have a notion that my voice told what I was feeling.

"Walter!" she said, as if surprised. "No, Kitty; why should he?"

"I—don't know. I only—only thought he might," I said, stumbling over the words. "He seemed to think—at least he said——"

"That would be a needless expense—no object in it," said she. "My illness has cost us enough already. Walter is hard at work, I hope——" and she made a little stop, as if she didn't feel

quite sure. "Hard at work, I hope," said she
again. "He ought not to think of another break
before Christmas."

"There's Michaelmas," I said.

I saw her give a little shake of the head, dark as
it was getting.

"Perhaps you'll come to Claxton at Christmas?"
I said; and all at once there were tears running
down my face. Mary couldn't see them—and even
if she did, she would only think it was because of her
going away.

"Hardly," she said. "No, that is very unlikely.
Walter and I have to be careful now about every
penny we spend. I think we shall have a snug
Christmas together at home this year." Then she
stooped to kiss me—she was the tallest, you know.
"Kitty, you must be brave," says she. "You and
I will feel very much being parted, after so many
weeks together, and I shall miss your mother sorely.
But we have to be brave, dear. After all, though
friendship brings with it the pain of saying good-
bye, one wouldn't be without the friendship, would
one?"

"No," I said; and I was thinking of Mr. Russell.
I was so glad she took my distress as having only
to do with herself—if she really did, which I have
my doubts about now. I've a notion she and
mother thought it was a case of "least said" about
her brother being "soonest mended."

We saw her off early in the afternoon of next
day; and oh, how I longed to send a message to

Mr. Russell; but I didn't dare. A word of remembrance would have been natural enough, only
I knew I could not say it without flushing up and
perhaps crying. And mother didn't speak of him
either. She never seemed to give him a thought,
no more than if there hadn't been such a person
alive. And father only said: "Mind, Mary, you are
to come again. You'll always be welcome." She
was "Mary" to all of us by then.

How strange the house did look without her!
She had grown to be part of it, part of ourselves;
and I didn't guess how much I loved her till she
was gone, nor what a gap her quiet face would
leave.

Mother was more silent than usual that afternoon, and hardly said a word about Mary going.
I wondered at first, knowing how fond those two
had grown of each other. Then when mother had
to speak about putting the bed upstairs again out
of the parlour, she choked, and couldn't go on for
a minute.

"I'm a stupid," says she. "Kitty, you run off
and get a blow on the common. That'll do you
good, and when you come back I'll be myself again.
I'll make you a cup of tea, and then you needn't
hurry," says she. "Father won't be in till late
to-day."

"But you'll be dull, mother," I said.

"I don't know as there's any harm in being
dull," says she. "When it comes in the way of
one's duty, I mean. Folks have got to go through

dull times, as well as lively times; and maybe they're none the worse after."

"Only, if I stay in——" said I.

"That's no good," says she. "Two dull folks don't make one cheerful one, however much they're mixed. You put on the kettle, sharp, and cut a slice of bread-and-butter. Yes; you've got to eat that; it don't matter whether you want to eat or don't want; and then you'll go and get a big bunch of wild-flowers. Mind you don't sit on the grass and brood."

It was late in the afternoon before I set off, and I didn't walk fast. A sort of tiredness was on me those days, and not caring much for anything; so I hadn't the spirit to run and be gay, as I'd have done a few weeks back. I loitered through the village, finding my way to the common by slow degrees, and then I loitered round it, getting ragged-robins out of the hedge, and blue speedwells, and meadow-sweet.

For a good while I kept near that part of the common where the big village boys were playing cricket; but presently I left them behind, and got away to a lonelier part.

. The sun was low by that time, shining with a yellow light through the branches of the trees; for there were many trees scattered about by ones or twos, and in little clumps, divided by open spaces.

I liked to feel myself alone, to know that nobody was watching me. If mother hadn't said what she did, I should have sat down on the grass

and given myself over to thinking—not of Mary
mostly, though I did feel her going, but of her
brother. I could always sit and think of Walter
Russell, for any time, and never want to be disturbed. It's wonderful how little I thought of poor
Rupert in those days.

But I knew mother would question me when I
got home; so I walked on, till I was so tired I
had to stop. And then I stood, leaning against the
trunk of an old elm, with the sunbeams shining
full on me, and a gold light all over the grass. It
was a pretty evening; one of the prettiest I have
ever seen.

I wondered what Mary was doing just then.
She would have reached home some time before,
—the little home she had often described to me,
till I seemed to know every corner of it. Most
likely she had unpacked and put everything away,
and she and her brother would be sitting down for
a long talk together, one on each side of the round
table in their parlour.

How happy they would be! He was such a
kind good brother, and Mary so devoted to him.
She might sometimes find fault with " Walter,"
but she loved him with all her heart. I didn't
think that any wonder either.

So happy together: talking, smiling, laughing,
telling everything that had happened, making merry
little jokes. Yes, I could picture it all! And I,
out there on the common, away from them both, felt
so lonely.

These thoughts were filling my mind, and I think I sighed more than once, with the longing to see Mr. Russell again.

I had shut my eyes, that I might the better picture those two in their parlour. Something made me open my eyes—I don't know what, unless it was the sound of a step on the grass, which I could not have said I heard—but I looked up.

And he was there; in front of me!

For a moment I felt stupefied, dazed! I couldn't believe what I saw. I couldn't believe he was Mr. Russell himself.

He said "Kitty!"

And then I had no more doubt.

CHAPTER VI.

THE EARL'S GIFT.

" Kitty ! " says he. " Why, Kitty, don't you know me ? "

I think I said " Oh ! " It didn't seem as if any other words would come at first. Such a rush of joy filled my heart, that I was almost afraid to look up in his face. I didn't want him to see all I felt. But I believe he did.

" Poor little Kitty ! " said he. " So you are glad to see me, eh ? "

" Oh—glad ! " I said, and stopped again.

" And I'm glad to see you. So we're even there," said he.

I wonder now that the words could satisfy me : yet they did.

" How ever did you come here ? " I asked him.

" How ? Why, by train part of the way, and the rest I walked," said he. " No, I didn't come to Claxton Station. I wanted a word with you, and nobody else. I should have been too well known at Claxton Station." Then he stood and looked at me. " Kitty, you are prettier than ever," says he. " You dear little thing ! I've never seen a lovelier girl. No, never. When I saw you just now, with your back against the tree in the sunshine, you looked just like a little angel," says he.

I suppose it was natural I should be pleased with this rubbish, being, as I was, only a silly girl, and nothing at all of the angel in me. I might have told him it wasn't, to my knowledge, the way of angels to stand leaning against tree-trunks, doing nothing. But I only dropped my eyes, and felt happy.

"Just like a little angel," says he again.

"I like you to think me pretty," I said, in a whisper. And then, with a start, I went on: "But you are too late. Mary is gone."

"Yes, I know," said he. "If I'd come to see Mary, I should have come to Claxton Station, and not have walked six miles for nothing."

I'd forgotten that for the moment.

"Kitty, I mustn't stay long," said he. "I've something very particular to say, and I've got to make haste and be off."

Such an unhappy look came over his face as he spoke. I was facing the sun, and he had his back to it; but even so I couldn't help seeing his look nor how pulled and haggard he was. It flashed on me that something had happened, and I was frightened, thinking at once of Mary.

"I've not seen Mary yet," said he, when I asked. "I have been away for hours. I couldn't see her till I had seen you first. The fact is, Kitty, I'm in dreadful trouble, and if you can't help me nobody can."

"Oh, what can I do? I would do anything," I cried. "Then doesn't Mary know you are here?"

"Nobody knows," said he. "I left word I meant to be home as early as I could. But I don't know, I'm sure, whether ——"

"Then she is all alone there," I said, thinking how I had pictured the two making merry together.

"Yes, I suppose so," said he. "It can't be helped. I meant to catch you earlier somehow, and I couldn't. I was watching from the hill, and I saw you go out, and come this way, so I went round and got to the common too. But it was ever so long before I could find you."

"And if you hadn't found me at all?" I said, wondering.

"Then——" and he stopped. "But I have—so that doesn't matter," says he. "Kitty, I want your help."

"What help? I'd do anything to help you," I said.

"Anything! Would you?" says he.

"Anything except what's wrong," I said. "And you wouldn't ask that."

"No, no, of course not," said he, in a hasty way, not looking at me. "Of course not."

"What do you want me to do?" I asked.

"Why," he said, "the fact is, I've got myself into an awful muddle, and I don't know how in the world to get out of it."

"Can't Mary help you?" I said.

"I wouldn't tell Mary for the world," says he. "I'd sooner never see her again."

It seemed very strange to me. I didn't like to think how strange it was. For surely the natural way would have been to tell his trouble to Mary, who had been sister, mother, friend, everything to him. And yet the very thought of his turning to me was a joy that made my heart flutter and the whole place seem bright. I didn't so much trouble myself with thinking what the "muddle" was that he had got into. He wanted *me* to help him! That was the joy.

"Don't say that," I begged. "Mary is so sweet and good."

"Mary is goodness itself," he said. "But she has a hard side. You haven't seen Mary yet in one of her stern moods, sitting in judgment on a poor chap."

I wouldn't have believed that Mary ever sat in judgment on anybody, if they had been any lips except Walter Russell's that said it. But I could not contradict him.

"What is it I can do for you?" I asked, and I looked up in his face. "Tell me!" I said.

"Kitty, you are a little angel," he exclaimed again, and most likely I blushed.

"Well, but tell me," I said. "It'll be getting late soon."

"So it will, and I haven't a moment to spare," says he. "Kitty ——" and there he stuck.

"Yes. What is it?" said I.

"Kitty, I want——" said he.

I couldn't help thinking of Rupert asking me to marry him, and a wonder came whether, perhaps—— But no, I could see it wasn't that with Mr. Russell. Being in a "muddle" couldn't mean that he was going to try to get a wife.

"Yes, you want what?" said I, to encourage him.

"I want—money," he blurted out at last.

I won't say it wasn't a blow. Somehow I had never thought of his coming to me for money. It seemed so odd. I couldn't help a sort of feeling that he lowered himself by it.

"Kitty, don't you misunderstand me," says he earnestly, seeing, I suppose, that my face fell. "I wouldn't have you think ill of me, Kitty, for anything. It's just a thing that I—that I can't help, you know. And I don't know where to turn; so I felt I must come to you. The truth is, I've been very much pressed; you know, Mary's illness has been such a pull, and I—well, in fact, I had to borrow a small sum. Only a small sum for a short time, just to tide me over a time of difficulty. And it has to be repaid now, and I don't know how to repay it. Don't you misunderstand me, Kitty," says he, and he looked at me so soft and kind that my silly little heart beat fast, and I felt I would do anything for him.

"Only I have no money!" I said.

"No; but I thought——" said he, and stopped.

"If only I could! I haven't five shillings of my own," I said. "Shall I ask father?"

"No, no! not for the world," says he. "Not a word to him nor anybody. Promise me you'll keep it quiet, Kitty! Promise."

"I won't say a word without you give me leave," I said, not at the moment thinking how I was making a second wrong promise; and yet I ought to have thought. He had a strange hold upon me, and I was willing to be in his power. I didn't want to break loose.

"That's my own little Kitty!" said he, and my heart bounded again with joy at the words.

"But I don't see what I am to do for you," I said. "Won't the person you have borrowed from wait a bit, till you can save up enough to pay him back?"

"Why, no; you don't exactly understand," says he. "It's not exactly that, you see—not exactly borrowing from a person."

"Not a person!" said I, wondering, and he gave a laugh.

"Why, no. Properly speaking, it's only using what I've got."

"I don't think I know what you mean," I said.

"No, I was sure you didn't,"—and he laughed again. "Only just that I'm in need of the money. That's enough too!"

I didn't speak, I felt so puzzled; and, after a minute, he burst out—

"Well, I'd best make a clean breast of it! I

H

can trust you, Kitty. Not a word 'll go a step farther, I know that! I can trust you, as I wouldn't any other living creature."

And I was foolish enough to be pleased at his saying so.

"You see, it really isn't exactly borrowing," he went on. "The fact is, a lot of money comes through my hands—children's school-pence, and so on—and I've got to account for it all. It's paid to me, and I've got a right to do as I like till the day I have to pay it over, which isn't just yet. But Mary is awfully fussy about such things, poor dear! and she always will have every penny put straight into a cash-box and kept apart. Well, she made me promise I'd go on the same while she was at your house; and I did mean—but somehow I got so close run, I couldn't, and I had to spend it all. The thing doesn't matter in itself; of course, I shall pay up all right when the proper time comes, but there'll be such a row when Mary finds her beloved cash-box empty! That's where it is, you see! I want to put in the money all right before I give it back to her. There's another purse, with money put by for the rent, and I had to borrow some of that too, for I was short, and I couldn't write and bother her. It's not borrowing really, you see, for what's hers is mine. Only I know there'll be a dreadful rumpus when she finds out. You haven't a notion how hard Mary can be!" He gave a sigh as he spoke. "She's a good creature, but she can be hard and no mistake;

and somehow she never has any mercy on me. So now you understand why I've come to you, eh? I knew you wouldn't be hard, Kitty," says he.

If I did "understand" it was with blinded eyes. I would not have any shadow cast upon my idol. I would not let myself take in what all this truly meant.

"Kitty, you see, don't you?" says he again. "I've nobody to go to except you. It's just a few pounds I want, just to tide me over this pinch. Only a loan, not a gift. I'll repay it faithfully. I declare I will."

"But—— " I said.

"No, you haven't the money, of course," said he. "But I've been thinking, there's something else you have, which wouldn't be missed for a few days—something one might raise a few pounds on, only for the moment, you know. It seems such a shame to think of such a thing, and if I wasn't in desperation what to do I would not! Still, if you didn't mind—if it were possible, just to save me from ruin and disgrace, and poor Mary from a broken heart, not to say another illness—yet I'm sure I don't know how to ask it of you. I really don't."

I was so bewildered, I stood and looked, wondering whatever he could mean.

"Don't you understand yet?" said he, his face falling.

"No," I said. "Something that I have!"

"Your watch!" says he, half in a whisper.

"My watch!" I said; and what he meant began to dawn on me. It made me feel queer, I can tell you.

"If you could, just for a few days or so," said he, and he spoke pleading-like. "Is that so very much to do for a friend, Kitty? It's only the loan I ask. You see, I could raise a few pounds on that watch, for the moment, just to tide me through; and then in a few days or so I would buy it back all right from the—the jeweller—and get it back to you. There'll be money coming in soon, one way and another, only I can't wait for that. If I haven't a few pounds *now*, either to-night or to-morrow morning, I don't know whatever I'm to do. I can't stand telling Mary, and that's flat. If I can't get the money, I can't go home, and then you'll never see nor hear of me again, Kitty!"

I felt a cold chill all through me at the thought.

"Oh, don't say that, please don't!" I begged. "It sounds too dreadful. I do wish you hadn't used up the money."

"Why, Kitty, as if I hadn't the right!" says he, quite short.

But had he the right? For strictly the money was not his. If he knew himself to have the right, and to be doing right, why should he mind speaking out to Mary? I tried not to see this, for I didn't want to blame him.

"I would lend you the watch for a few days," I said; "only I don't know what father and mother would say."

" They mustn't know, of course," said he. " You've promised not to tell, not to let slip a word."

" Yes," I said. That promise was lying heavy on my conscience. " But if they asked me to fetch the watch and to show it to anybody ? "

" Oh, they won't. I dare say it doesn't happen once in six weeks."

" I don't think it's so seldom as once in six weeks, and it might be any day," I said.

" But you don't wear it commonly ? "

" No," I said.

" Oh, well, it'll all come right," says he. " They won't speak of it, or if they do, you must just put them off somehow. You can say you can't find it, and that'll be true enough. Only mind you don't let out where it is."

The marvel is that my eyes weren't opened. For wasn't it plain as daylight that he cared not a rap about my feelings, but only for his own ? So long as he could get things straight for himself, *I* might have any amount of worry and difficulty. Besides, there was the untruthfulness of what he wanted me to do. He might be sure that I should find myself obliged either to betray him or to deceive.

He knew I wouldn't betray him. That meant that he expected me to deceive.

But he had got the mastery of me, with his soft looks, and his threat that I might never see him again. I had given in to temptation earlier for his sake, so it was doubly hard to conquer now. I

hardly thought of conquering. My one wish was
to help him. That came first, and the question of
doing right or wrong came second.

"Kitty, will you save me?" he asked. "Will
you save me from——" and he stopped. "From
Mary!" says he.

And I was overcome. I burst into tears and
said "Yes."

He told me I was an angel again, and said a
lot of absurd things. Then he comforted me, and
said I mustn't cry, for "all would be right now,"
and he hoped very soon to come again. I asked,
"When?" and he said, "Oh, very soon indeed—
in fact, it must be soon, for he would have to bring
back the watch."

"Please don't be long about .that," I begged.
"Father thinks so much of the Earl giving it to
me, you know. I don't know what I shall do if
he finds out."

"Oh, he won't find out. There's no fear," Mr.
Russell said. "You've just got to shirk the sub-
ject. But I shan't be long. I'll just turn up with
it as I've done to-day."

"In a week?" I wanted to know.

"Oh, well, perhaps in a week or two," says he.

"It's only the watch you want, not the chain
too?" I said.   .

"Why, I don't see the good of dividing them,"
said he. "And they mightn't be willing to give
me—lend me, I mean—quite enough on the watch.
I'd better have both."

I made no resistance. Having let him take his own way so far, he had matters in his hands, and I had only to obey.

He would not walk homeward with me, lest he should be seen; but we settled that I was to take the watch out into the garden after dark. And all the time I tried to hold myself from seeing how very very wrongly I was acting.

It didn't take me long to reach the station. Mother met me indoors with a smile, and I could see she was better for her quiet time. She told me I looked better too, and there's no doubt I was flushed, and not so tired.

"I didn't expect you to be so long, Kitty," said she. "But no matter, if it's done you good."

Another half-hour brought darkness, and the puzzle then was how to get away. I had slipped the watch and chain into my dress, all ready; and I was in a tremble of nervousness. Mother wanted me to settle down to some mending, and she seemed uncommon disposed for talk.

"Why, Kitty, you're all in a fidget," says she. "What's the matter?"

"I don't feel like sitting still," I said.

"No more did I, but it don't do to give in to that sort of thing," said she. "It's Mary's going: nought else. Saying good-bye does unsettle folks. But you've had your walk, and now you'd best be busy."

Mother got out her work, and took a chair opposite: so I knew she meant to keep me at it.

"I wonder what Mary is doing now," says she.

Poor Mary! I couldn't but wonder too, thinking of all those hours spent alone. And every minute that I put off seeing Mr. Russell kept him longer away from her!

"She is having a talk with her brother, I don't doubt," mother went on. "He's no favourite of mine, that young fellow, for I don't trust him; but all the same he's fond of Mary, and he'll give her a welcome. I shouldn't wonder if they're having a merry time together."

Mother hadn't spoken of him before, since I don't know when. It took me by surprise, and I said, "O mother, don't!"

"Why, Kitty!" says she. "Poor little woman! Can't you bear to speak of Mary yet?"

I couldn't bear to hear her spoken of so, knowing how different things really were. I would not let myself blame Walter Russell, yet I could have no happy thoughts of him, after what had passed. For a minute I tried to keep on at my needle, but it was no use. I couldn't; and I just dropped the work and went to the window, where it was grown too dark to see anything outside.

Mother said nothing at first. She let me stand there for awhile; and when all at once I walked to the door, she only asked — "What now, Kitty?"

"I'm going for a turn outside," I said. "It's quite warm."

"Yes, so it is; but put on my shawl, and don't

stay," says she. "Just leave the fidgets behind you, and come back."

The moment I had shut the door I set off running, and reached the back corner of the garden, where Mr. Russell had said he would wait for me, close to the lilac bushes. I was barely able to see him, and I said "Mr. Russell!" under my breath.

"I thought you didn't mean to come at all," says he, in a whisper.

"I couldn't sooner," I said; "and I mustn't wait now." Then I put the gold watch and chain into his hands. "Take care of them, please!" I begged. "And oh, please don't keep them long! I shall be so frightened till I have them safe again."

"Not a minute longer than I can help," says he. "Good-bye, little Kitty—I can't thank you enough. You've saved me from no end of bother," says he.

Then he was gone, making no sound, but stealing off like somebody in disgrace; and I went back with a heart as heavy as lead. I knew I had let him draw me into a tangle of wrong-doing, out of which I could see no way of escape. I could only rest my hopes on his promise not to keep the watch long.

As I had told Mr. Russell, it was not so seldom as only once in six weeks that I had to show the Earl's present to somebody. Still, for some time past the watch had been allowed to lie undisturbed;

and it didn't seem likely I should be called upon in a hurry. Most friends in the neighbourhood had seen it; and father wasn't one to make a great fuss and talk about the matter.

But only two days after I had parted with the watch I found myself in difficulties.

Mother had a note from Mary that morning by post: a short note, saying that she was at home, and sent love to us all. She spoke gratefully of all the kindness we had shown her, but she never mentioned her brother. I could not understand this: for the note was written next day after she left us, so of course he was at home with her. Mother seemed puzzled too, though not exactly about that.

"Mary is in trouble," she said. "I wish I knew what is wrong."

Well, in the afternoon of that same day, Mr. Armstrong came to call. That was nothing un-usual; but he had a lady with him, a stranger to the place. The moment I saw them walking up the garden-path I had a sort of sinking with fright, for I guessed what would follow.

If I could have run away, I would have made my escape. It was no use to think of that, though. I should only have met them at the door, as I went out; and besides, I was holding a big skein of grey yarn for mother to wind, which kept me fast to the spot.

Father had just come in with a newspaper in his hand, and he had sat down to read it.

Mr. Armstrong was sure of a welcome in our house. He had been a kind friend to us for many a long day.

Mother laid aside the grey wool, and set a chair for the lady, while I got another for Mr. Armstrong. He told us he had brought his sister-in-law, Mrs. Withers, to make our acquaintance; and then he thanked me for the chair, shaking hands. "Why, Kitty," said he, "you don't look well, child. What's the matter?" For indeed the fright had made me queer.

"Kitty don't seem just as she should be lately," mother said. "She has a sort of turn like that once in a way. Sit down, Kitty," says she.

I did as mother told me, trying not to let them see how I shook, and getting a little less frightened as the minutes went by, and they only talked of things in general.

"So your invalid has gone at last," Mr. Armstrong said to mother.

"Yes," said she; "and sorry we are to lose her. There's not many folks like Mary Russell."

"I am sure of that," said he. "She carries her goodness in her face."

"It's genuine out-and-out goodness too," father said. "Why, now, she's been like a mother to that young brother of hers."

"And he is grateful for it?" Mr. Armstrong spoke as if he was putting a question, not as if he was sure.

"No doubt," says father.

" He talks gratitude," mother says quite low.

" But doesn't act it, perhaps," Mrs. Withers said.

" Talk is easier than action, any day," Mr. Armstrong added, with a smile.

" Yes, sir. I can't abide talk," mother answered him.

" You don't like talk of the wrong sort," says Mr. Armstrong.

" It's sure to be wrong, when there's much of it," says mother.

" Too often, I'm afraid—yes," Mr. Armstrong said. " 'In the multitude of words there wanteth not sin,' you know."

" That's just it," mother said.

And then what I was dreading came all of a sudden.

" Mrs. Phrynne, I saw a friend of yours last week," says Mr. Armstrong.

Mother waited to hear more.

" I mean Lord Leigh," said he.

" His lordship wouldn't thank you to call him my friend," says mother.

" I'm not so sure," says Mr. Armstrong, smiling. " He asked most particularly after you and Kitty, and he said he wished there were more mothers like you in the world."

" I'm much obliged to him, sir," mother said; and though she tried not to look too pleased, she was pleased.

" And that reminds me," says Mr. Armstrong, " I want Mrs. Withers to see the Earl's present to your Kitty—the famous gold watch. Would you have any objection ? "

"Not a bit," says father. "Run and fetch it, Kitty."

I got up and went, though going was no good. At least it would give me time to think what I was to say or do. It's a wonder they didn't all see how dazed I was, and how I could scarce stand, for my knees were knocking together; but somehow they didn't. Father was talking to Mr. Armstrong; and mother was listening to Mrs. Withers · and nobody happened to look.

I can't explain the sort of odd feeling that crept over me—a feeling as if I really had to look for the watch, even while it was no manner of use. I walked upstairs to my room, going slow because I couldn't go fast; and I opened the drawer where I always kept the watch, and peeped into other drawers as well. It must have been a temptation to deceit, though at the moment I seemed to do it in a sort of natural way.

Then I went to the glass, and saw my own face, without a scrap of colour, and the lips all yellow-white. I didn't wonder; I felt so shaky and sick.

What would they say downstairs? What would they think? How could I keep from saying what wasn't true and yet shelter Mr. Russell ?

"But I mustn't betray him ! I have promised ! Nobody is to know !" I said aloud.

I didn't dare to go back, though I knew they were expecting me. I stood leaning against the table, counting the moments, in a sort of dull, half-stupid state. Perhaps if I waited long enough, Mr. Armstrong would get tired, and go away.

All at once father shouted "Kitty!"

I said "Yes," so as he couldn't possibly have heard.

"Kitty, make haste!" he called again. ".What are you after, child? Come along!"

There was no help for it. I had to go. I went downstairs step by step, holding on to the banisters. As soon as father saw me, he said—"Make haste, child!" and went back to the others; so I had to follow alone.

Mr. Armstrong was the first to catch sight of my face. "Why, Kitty! what is wrong?" says he. "The child is ill, surely."

Father got hold of me, and the next moment I was sobbing as if my heart would break.

They were all in a puzzle at first. Mother thought I was taken sick, and Mrs. Withers brought out a bottle of smelling-salts. Father seemed to understand better, for I heard him say, —"Something is worrying the child."

"It's Mary's going," mother answered. "She hasn't been right ever since."

"Well, but that wouldn't make her cry like this, all in a moment," says father. "What is it, Kitty? Eh, dear? Don't you feel well?—or anything gone wrong?"

" Come, cheer up, Kitty," Mr. Armstrong said.
" You'll see Mary again soon, I don't doubt. Come,
where is the pretty watch you were going to show
us ? "   I suppose he thought that would take my
thoughts off my trouble, whatever it was.

" Yes, where's the watch, Kitty ? " says father.

I managed to get out—" It—it—isn't there ! "
and cried harder than before. The crying wasn't
put on ; for I did feel it to be dreadful that I
should deceive them all like this.

" Not there ! You don't mean to say the watch
is gone ! " father exclaimed.

" Kitty, you must tell us plainly. Is the watch
gone ? Cannot you find it ? " Mr. Armstrong
asked gravely.

" No," I sobbed.

" Where did you look ? In the place where you
always keep it ? Anywhere else ? " father asked.

" I know where Kitty keeps it. I'll go and
look," mother said.

She was gone some minutes, and they put
more questions, while I hid my face, and said as
little as I possibly could. Father seemed very
troubled, and so did Mr. Armstrong. It would
be a grievous thing, Mr. Armstrong said, if such a
theft had taken place. He could not help hoping
that I had merely mislaid the watch.

" That don't seem likely either," father said.
" Kitty wouldn't let the watch lie about anywhere."

" When did you have it out last, Kitty ? " Mr.
Armstrong asked.

I could say truly that I had held it in my hands a few days ago.   But when Mr. Armstrong questioned whether I was quite sure I had put it safely back, I burst into fresh crying, and couldn't answer him.

Then mother came back, looking downright pale with worry.

"No," she said; "the watch isn't in its right place, nor anywhere else that I can see.   We'll have a turn-out of every corner, before I go to bed to-night.   But I'm very much afraid—— " and she stopped.   "Though who could be the thief I haven't a notion."

CHAPTER VII.

THE SEARCH.

MOTHER was as good as her word. She didn't leave a corner of the house unsearched. There wasn't a cupboard, nor a drawer, nor a box that she didn't empty. But of course it was no good.

I was poorly enough all the evening to have a good excuse for not helping her. Not being strong, any sort of worry was apt to put me into an ailing state. Nobody wondered that I was worried at the watch being gone: though mother did tell me I needn't cry so every time it was spoken about, or a question was asked me. I couldn't help the crying, for I felt downright miserable; and, besides, it was a sort of protection. If I hadn't cried, I should have had to answer a lot more questions; and so, as was natural, the tears came.

As for helping mother in her search, I couldn't, and that's the long and short of it. I hadn't the face to go about turning out drawers, and pulling everything upside down, when all the while I knew where the watch was. At least, if I didn't exactly know where the watch was just then, I knew in what direction it had gone, and how one might hear of it.

Another thought had come to me, which somehow I hadn't got hold of before. I didn't see how in the world I was ever to get out of the muddle I was in.

Supposing Mr. Russell brought back the watch in a week or two, as he had promised—and as I tried to feel sure he would—what was I to say to father and mother?

Was I to pretend I had stumbled upon it somewhere by accident, and make up a story of where it had been hidden? But that would be a carrying on of miserable deceit, a course of evil through and through. Was I just to bring it out, and obstinately refuse to answer any questions? But that would puzzle everybody, and be a great distress to father and mother. Then what *was* I to do? I couldn't see my way at all.

When mother had come to the end of her hunting, she walked into the parlour—we had the use of our little parlour again, which was the only good thing to do with Mary's going—and she says, "It's the most extraordinary thing I ever heard of."

"It's a case of thieving, I'm afraid," father said. He looked bothered, for he had valued the Earl's gift not a little, and no wonder.

"I shall have to put it in the hands of the police," said he; "and the sooner the better." So he got up. "I'll wire to-night for one to come

in the morning," said he; for we hadn't a policeman actually living in Claxton, though there was
one who went to and fro through the place as part
of his beat.

That terrified me. I had a notion that the
police could always ferret out anything; and the
thought of the questions which a policeman would
ask me, and which I should have to answer, was
too dreadful. I started up out of my chair and
cried—

"O father, don't!"

"Don't—what?" says he.

"Don't go to the police," I begged. "Please,
please don't, father!"

Father almost laughed, for all he was so worried.

"Why, you little goose of a kittenkins," said
he; and then he patted me on the cheek. "Don't
you want to get the watch back? For if you
don't, I do."

But I could only say, "Please, please don't."

"Why not?" said he.

And I hung my head, and muttered, "He'll ask
such a lot of questions."

"He'll be bound to do that," father said. "The
more he asks, the better, so as he finds the watch.
Why, Kitty, what's come over you to-day?"

"I shan't be able to answer him—I know I
shan't," I said. "I shall be so—so———"

"So what?" says father.

"So frightened," I said. "O father, don't—
please don't send for a policeman."

"One would think the child had made away with the watch herself," father said; and all this time mother stood watching us in her silent way. "I declare I wouldn't have believed you hadn't more sense, Kitty. Frightened at a policeman! I never heard of such a thing."

Then he patted my cheek again, and gave it a kiss.

"Come, come, Kitty, you've cried enough for one day," says he. "We won't have any more nonsense. It's a trouble losing the watch, no doubt about that; but we don't blame our Kitty. Somebody's managed to steal in, and to walk off with it, and we've got to find that somebody. I shall send for a policeman, of course: why shouldn't I? The thief isn't going to get off so easy, I can tell him! It wouldn't be right for me not to act; and what's more, it wouldn't be right for the sake of other people. And as for the policeman's questions, you just take your time, and answer him slow, and don't get into a flurry. Take care you tell him the very exact truth, and not a word more nor less. That's all you've got to do, and then you'll have no call to be frightened."

But to tell "the very exact truth, and not a word more nor less," was the trouble; for there was my promise to Mr. Russell; and more than the promise, there was my wish to shield him from blame. More than the promise, I say; for if it came to a question of breaking that promise, or telling a lot of other lies, I'm sure I should have done best in breaking that promise. One crooked step had landed me where a straight step was hardly possible, and the quickest way out of the coil was the wisest. But I couldn't bear to think of bringing blame to him.

It's hard to say, in such a coil, what one ought or ought not to do. Only, there's no doubt I had given a promise which I had no right to give; and my father and mother had a right to hear the whole. All the same, it's a terrible thing to break through one's pledged word. I've learnt from those days how slow folks ought to be to pledge their word, and how wrong hasty promises are. "Least said, soonest mended," you know.

Father went away, leaving me in tears, and mother came to the table. She didn't speak at first. She had such a fashion of weighing her words. I remember how she smoothed the table-cloth, and put straight one or two books on it that had got awry. Then all of a sudden she said—

"Kitty, are you hiding anything from us about the watch?"

Mother's eyes had seen deeper than father's. Such an idea hadn't come to him. The words seemed to take my breath, for I didn't know what to say. I remembered again that I had to shelter Mr. Russell, and I saw that if I went on crying like this, I should not be able. People would begin to suspect.

She didn't put the question again, but waited,

standing quiet, and I dried my eyes and tried to be more cheerful.

"If only father wouldn't have a policeman!" I said. "It does seem so horrid—a policeman hunting all over our rooms. And I don't believe it'll do any good."

"You nor I can't judge of that," mother said.

"If father was to speak to people, and advertise," I said—feeling that I must talk, or mother would ask again the question I hadn't answered.

"Advertise for the thief to bring back stolen goods!" Mother gave a little laugh. "Kitty, have you taken leave of your senses?" says she.

"I do hate the thought of a policeman coming," I said.

"Maybe it's not what we would have chosen," said she. "But if I'm willing, you needn't worry. Don't you think father knows best how to manage?"

We didn't go on talking, and mother let alone the question she had put; but I knew she hadn't forgotten it.

At family prayers that evening father read the chapter in Acts about Ananias and Sapphira: not by choice, for it came in regular order. I couldn't help shivering as I listened; and when we got up from prayers, father said—

"That's a fearful chapter, isn't it? I always think so, every time I read it. Shows so plain what God thinks of untruth. And it wasn't even as if Ananias had told a downright outspoken lie. It was just shuffling and deceiving."

I thought over those words of father's, lying in bed, and pictured the awful end of husband and wife, struck dead in the very act and word of falsehood. I couldn't bear to remember the untruths I had already been led into, and I made up my mind that I would not say another word that wasn't true. I would only refuse to answer, and take the consequences.

But it is no easy matter, if one steps down into evil, to keep one's self from going farther than just a certain point.

The policeman came next morning: a tall man, with a grave face, almost as sparing of his words as mother. He listened to the whole story from father, and then he went upstairs to see my room, paying particular attention to the way of getting there. He looked into the drawer where I had always kept the watch, and made mother turn everything out that was in it; and then he examined the other drawers, as if to make sure that I hadn't slipped it in elsewhere by mistake. He put a question now and then to mother by the way, and I waited in a fright, knowing my turn must come soon, as indeed it did.

"Quite sure you always kept the watch and chain in this drawer?" says he at last, looking at me.

"Yes," I said, under my breath.

"Speak out, Kitty. Don't be afraid," says father.

"And the drawer wasn't locked?" says the policeman.

"No."

"Never?"

"No," I said.

"Anybody except yourselves know where the watch was kept?"

"No."

"Yes," mother put in; "Mary Russell knew." Mother gave a little laugh. "But she is one of ourselves."

The policeman wanted to know all about Mary—who she was, where she lived, how long she had been with us, when she had left. Mother answered these questions; and the name of Walter came in too. I wouldn't say a word.

"Then the watch was missed two days after she left?" says the policeman.

Mother smiled.

"Oh, you needn't think anything of that," says she. "I'd as soon suspect myself as Mary Russell—if not sooner. We know her well."

The policeman didn't look quite so certain, but he only asked—

"What about the young fellow, her brother?"

"A schoolmaster: clever young fellow, and most respectable every way," father declared.

"Didn't know where the watch was, of course?" says the policeman.

Mother said "No," and so did I; but I could see the policeman's mind to be hankering after Mr. Russell.

"When was he here last?" says he.

I wanted mother to answer, but neither she nor father spoke, and I had to say—

"He went away a whole month before his sister."

"Never been to the place since?"

"Not to my knowledge," said mother; but the policeman kept looking at me, and I couldn't help my colour getting up.

"Never been since?" said he.

"He meant to come and fetch his sister—but he—didn't!" I said, almost whispering. In a sort of way that was true, for sure enough he hadn't been to fetch Mary. But, on the other hand, it was not true, for I was trying to make the policeman think that he had not been at all, when he had been.

The policeman made an odd sort of a click with his tongue.

"When did you see your watch last?" says he.

"Not long——" I said.

"How long ago?"

"Just a few days."

"How many days?" says he, as determined as could be.

"The day Mary Russell went," I said.

"That's three days ago," says father. "Why, Kitty, you didn't tell us that," says he. "I thought it was ever so much longer."

"Did you see the watch last before that young woman left, or after she was gone?" says the policeman.

"After," I said; and I heard mother give a sort of sigh of relief.

" Sure ? "

" Yes," I said.

"What hour did the young woman leave?" says he.

" Two-fifty-five train," mother said. " We saw her off ourselves."

"And you saw the watch—when?" says the policeman to me.

" A good deal later," I told him. " After I came in from a walk."

" What hour ? " says he again.

" I don't know—exactly," I said, though I could have told pretty near. I was frightened at all this questioning.

" When you went to take off your hat?" says mother.

I said " Yes."

" Then it couldn't have been before six," says she. " I know it wasn't long after you were in before it got dark, for you didn't sit many minutes over your work, before you took a turn in the garden, and it was dark then."

" Took a turn in the garden after dark ! " says the policeman, and he had his eyes on me.

" She was upset about Mary Russell going, and wanted a breath of air," mother said. " I spoke about Mary, and she couldn't stand it."

" Had a walk just before," says the policeman.

" Yes. She wasn't five minutes in the garden," says mother.

"And when you saw the watch," says the policeman to me, "was between the walk and the five minutes in the garden, eh? When you went upstairs to take off your hat, eh?"

I said "Yes."

"You didn't take the watch into the garden with you?"

Here was the point where the real pull came. If I said "Yes," how could I shield Walter? The temptation was too much for me, and no wonder, for I'd put myself in the way of it, and couldn't look to be kept from evil.

"No," I said, under my breath.

But I had waited a moment, and the colour came red and hot to my face. The policeman looked hard at me.

"You saw the watch just before you went into the garden," says he. "How did you happen to see it? Did you open the drawer?"

"Yes," I said.

"On purpose to look at the watch?"

"Yes."

"And you took it out, and handled it?"

"Yes."

"And put it back in the drawer—watch and chain too?"

I couldn't answer him straight off; but after a moment's stop, I said "Yes" again. Another lie!

"Sure you didn't put on the watch and chain to wear?"

"No."

"Nor have them anywhere about you?"

"No," I said.

See how one falsehood dragged other falsehoods in its train, and how every untruth I spoke made it harder for me to go back! It's a horrible slippery road I was on. And it was Walter Russell, the man I loved, who had led me there!

"Then you can say positively that you left the watch and chain safe in your drawer that evening, three days ago, somewhere between six and seven o'clock?" says he.

And once more I said "Yes," though the word seemed to tear me in half, and my colour was gone, and a shivering came over me.

"You didn't look again in the drawer, nor miss the watch, till yesterday?"

I burst out sobbing, for I didn't know how to bear it, and said "No."

The policeman didn't ask any more; he turned and went downstairs with father and mother. I stayed behind at first, but after a moment I thought I would go too, and I went to the top of the stairs, and there waited again, not certain what to do. The parlour door was wide open, and I could hear father saying—

"Well, what do you think of it?"

The policeman's answer was a deal lower, yet it came to me quite distinct—

"Mr. Phrynne, that girl of yours is not speaking the truth!"

"Eh! What! Kitty!" father exclaimed. "Why,

our Kitty has always been as open as the day— hasn't she, mother ?" says he.

But mother made no answer.

"True as steel," says father. "Poor little Kitty!"

I couldn't go down after that; and at the moment I couldn't make up my mind to go back into my room, though I knew it was mean and wrong to listen. But I didn't gain anything by it, for the parlour door was shut before any more was said.

So then I just sat down on the top stair, and leant my head against the banisters, and felt as if I didn't want ever to move or do anything again, I was so miserable.

I suppose being unhappy makes most people poorly. It always did me. When mother came upstairs a good while later, and found me there, I was so queer and sick, I could hardly stand.

She made me lie down on my bed, and brought me a cup of tea, and was so good, it went through me like an arrow to think how I was deceiving her and father. Mother wasn't used to turn stiff and cold in manner if she wasn't pleased, like some people; and she was never in a hurry to speak out; she could always bide her time. At all events, she didn't say a word to me that day which sounded like distrust. Of course she could not guess that I had overheard what the policeman had said.

I wasn't able to go down to dinner, and I lay on my bed all the afternoon, most of the time crying softly. Father was very busy—only just in to dinner, and out again.

A little before tea-time, mother came and said I had better go downstairs. I would rather have stayed where I was, for I felt afraid of everything and everybody; but it was no good to struggle against what mother thought best. So I got up, and found my way into the parlour, and managed it better than I had expected.

Tea was ready, and father sitting at the table. He didn't say much, except just to ask how I was; and there was a look in his face—which I couldn't remember seeing there before—a sort of pained disappointed look. Once or twice he sighed, and I saw mother glance across at him. He would talk a deal at tea-time commonly, and it was our brightest meal, mother seeming to like to listen, though she mightn't say much. But we had no talk that day, and if anybody said a word to me, I was ready to burst out crying.

After tea was done, mother took away the things to wash in the kitchen. She wouldn't let me help, but said I was to keep quiet, and presently she shut the door, leaving me alone with father.

He had got a book, and was reading while mother cleared the table. When she had done, and we two were alone together, he put down the book, and turned to look at me across the corner of the table.

"Better, Kitty?" said he.

"I don't know, father," I said.

"There don't seem to be enough in the loss of a watch to make you sick and unhappy," says he.

"It's a misfortune, and I'm sorry for it. That's all. Not worth breaking your heart about."

"No, father," I said in a whisper. If only that had been all!

"Kitty," says father suddenly, "I think you had best see Mr. Armstrong."

"See Mr. Armstrong, father!"

"Yes," said he. "I think maybe you'd tell Mr. Armstrong what you won't tell mother nor me."

I didn't suppose father meant more than just what I had heard the policeman say, and I answered—

"O no!—please!"

"There's something you've got to tell somebody, eh?"

"No, father," I said, all in a shake.

"Nothing at all?" says he. "Are you sure, Kitty—quite sure?"

Father reached across the table to pat my hand, and he spoke in his kindest tone, sorrowful, but not angry.

"No, father," I said.

"Nothing you're hiding from us, Kitty?"

I suppose it was easier to cry than to speak, and so I burst out sobbing again. But father didn't pay so much heed to the tears as he commonly did, for he was intent on what he had to say.

"Kitty, are you hiding something from mother and me?" says he. "Don't cry, but look me in the face, and tell me! Kitty"—and his voice wasn't steady—"Kitty, if you'll just look me in the face, and speak out, and tell me you're hiding nothing,

I'll believe you. I'd believe your word if things was ever so against you. Only look me straight in the face, and speak out firm and strong."

But I couldn't do that. For all the lies I had told, I *couldn't* look him in the face and tell another. I just sat and sobbed.

"Then there is something," says he to himself.

"I wish the watch had never been given me at all," says I.

"So do I too, if it's changed our Kitty like this," says father.

And then he made one more try. He pulled his chair nearer, and looked at me anxious-like, as I could see.

"I'm very much afraid there's something wrong," says he again. "I'm very much afraid you've not been altogether open and above-board. It don't matter why I think so, for I do. But it's not too late yet. If you'll speak out now, and tell the plain truth, mother and I will forgive what's wrong. We'll forgive, and we won't talk of it again. Won't you, Kitty? For your mother's sake and mine— and most of all for the sake of doing what's right, and pleasing to God. . . . You won't be happy going on so. . . . Kitty, haven't you a word to say to me? . . . Not one word!"

I sat still, staring down on the table-cloth, with a big lump in my throat, but making no sign.

"Won't you, Kitty?" says he once more.

But I made no answer still, for I didn't know what to say, and my tongue seemed stiff, as if it wouldn't stir. So then he got up and walked out of the room, and I heard him say to mother in such a heavy sad tone—

" No use! She won't speak ! "

Ah, if I had but spoken ! If I had but told him I was puzzled, and didn't know how to act! If I had but replied to his loving words and looks !

The moment he was gone, I wished with all my heart I had done differently : yet I didn't run after him. I was so afraid of being betrayed into letting slip about Walter Russell.

I didn't see father again that evening, for mother made me go to bed early, and in the morning she wouldn't let me come down to breakfast. When I did come down, father was gone to his work. He would be busier than usual, we knew, for there were a lot of excursion trains running that day having to do with some races a few stations off.

Mother seemed just the same as always in her manner, only she was so silent and so grave— silent even for her. She hardly opened her lips at all, and I could see a sort of grieved look: not vexed—only grieved. And I knew it was about me. I longed to tell her I was sorry; yet I said nothing.

I hadn't been downstairs an hour, when something took us both by surprise. Mother was washing up the breakfast china, and I was drying the cups, when all of a sudden the kitchen door leading into the garden was pushed gently open, and Mary Russell walked in.

K

Mother just said "Mary!" and I let slip the cup I held, so that it fell and was broken.

"No need for that either!" mother said.

Mary stood still, looking at us with such sorrowful eyes, and her face was more worn and pale than when she went away.   One could see she had had trouble or worry of some sort, since leaving us.

Mother picked up the three pieces of the cup, and put them on the table.   Then she went forward, and gave Mary a kiss.

"My dear, you're always welcome," she said. "But why didn't you tell us you were coming?"

"I didn't know—till——" Mary said.

"Till when?" mother asked.

"Till late last night."

"And you look as if you hadn't slept all night, neither," says mother.   "Sit down, and Kitty shall make you a cup of tea.   You must have had breakfast early."

"I didn't have any breakfast," Mary said, with a sort of smile.   "Nor any sleep, either."

"None at all!" says mother.

"I didn't go to bed.   I had a lot to think about."

"If I was you, I'd have thought about it lying down," says mother.   "That wasn't like your wisdom, Mary."

"Maybe not," Mary said, with a strange look. "But I've got to tell you——"

"You've got to tell me nothing till you've had some breakfast," says mother, making Mary take a seat. "There's boiling water all ready, and Kitty shall see to the tea sharp. Cut some bread and butter too, Kitty. No, I won't have you talk, Mary, till you've taken something. It isn't long to wait."

It mightn't be long to mother, but it was long to me. I wondered so, what *could* Mary be going to say? Was it about her brother? Had something happened to him? I didn't know how to bear the putting off, and I hurried all I could with the tea and bread and butter, so as I might hear the sooner.

Mary sat still, looking from mother to me. There was a pitying look in her eyes that I couldn't make out.

"Did you see my husband in the station, Mary?" mother asked, when I had brought the tea, and put it in front of Mary, and she had begun to sip.

Mary gave a sorrowful glance up in mother's face.

"Yes," she said; "I saw him at the further end of the platform. I didn't stop to speak to him, and he didn't see me. I thought I'd come here first."

Mother made no answer, and showed no haste to know why, and I felt half wild with impatience: yet I had just to go on drying the cups and saucers, for mother went back to her washing, and kept handing them to me. I couldn't think why mother didn't at least just ask if anything was wrong with Walter. But I didn't dare ask it myself.

"My husband has a lot to do to-day—all these excursion trains," mother said. "It's on account of the races."

"I came by an excursion train," says Mary.

"They don't all stop here, but some do," says mother. "He's got a deal to see to, and won't be in till dinner-time."

"No," Mary said, in a dreamy-like tone.

She was getting near the end of the last slice, and I watched her, as greedy as could be for her to have done, that I might hear what she had to say.

"Another slice, Mary?" says mother.

"O no, thank you. Not any more," says Mary.

"You're better for that, aren't you?" mother said.

"Yes—much, thank you."

"And you'll have a second cup of tea, my dear?"

"No; not any more. Nothing more at all," says Mary.

Mother had finished the washing up, and I was at the end of the drying. Mother carried away the wooden bowl, and emptied it, as quiet as if nothing at all out of the common was happening. She made me put away the china, and she rubbed the table dry; and all the time Mary sat watching, without a word, and I was in such a fret, I didn't know how to bear myself.

"Now," mother says at last, drawing down her

sleeves to her wrist; "now you've had something: so you're fit to speak, and I'm free to listen."

Mary looked up into mother's face, and then at me—oh, so sadly! I couldn't think whatever in the world she meant.

"If you'd rather Kitty should go——" says mother.

"No; Kitty may stay," says Mary.

And then we could just hear the ticking of the clock, the room was so still.

Mother stood with her eyes on Mary's face.

"My dear, you've had a lot of worry since you went," she said.

"Yes," Mary answered.

"And you're going to tell us all about it now, my dear."

But Mary didn't speak. I could see her lips working, in a way they had — not as if she wanted to cry, but as if she was troubled, and didn't know how to put into words what she had to say.

"It's something to do with your brother," mother says—not as if she was asking a question, but as if she was sure.

"Yes; it's something to do with Walter," says Mary; and how my heart did beat!

Then all of a sudden Mary turned to me.

"Kitty's not looking well," she said.

"No," says mother.

"Nor happy."

"No—nor happy," mother answered.

" And you've all been worried too, Mrs. Phrynne."

" Yes ; we've been worried," mother says quietly.

" About the lost watch ! " says Mary.

That did take us aback, both of us. I know I jumped as if I was shot, and mother says quite sharp—

"Why, Mary! how ever did you hear about that?"

" A friend of yours came yesterday, asking questions," says she.

" A friend ! Not the policeman ? "

" He was in plain clothes, but he was a policeman."

Mother had actually got tears in her eyes.

" I didn't mean you to have *that* bother, my dear," said she. " I didn't think the man would, after all I said."

" The man only did his duty," says Mary. " He was quite right to come. Walter was out; but I had a long talk with him. That was the first I heard of the watch being lost."

" And you're come to tell us you're sorry," says mother.

" Not only to say I am sorry," Mary answered.

A sudden stab seemed to go all through me from head to foot. I never felt anything like it before. I didn't half know where I was, nor what I was doing. For Mary drew out of her pocket a little rolled-up parcel, and laid it on the table, undoing the string. And when she opened the brown paper, there lay my gold watch and chain.

CHAPTER VIII.

FOUND OUT.

MOTHER didn't say a word. She sat down, and a queer grey look came over her face.

I stood leaning against the dresser, feeling—but I couldn't tell what I felt. All the wrong I had done, all the falsehoods I had spoken, had been for nothing. I hadn't even the poor little reward that I had sinned for! I had not shielded Walter from blame. Somehow or other the matter had come to light.

Mary said nothing either. She looked so sad, so pitying.

We couldn't all have kept silence many seconds, I suppose, but it seemed an age. Before anybody spoke, father walked in.

"I haven't a moment," says he cheerily, "but somebody tells me Mary Russell has come, and I wanted to make sure. Why, so she is! Well, Mary, how d'you——Hallo!"

For his eyes fell on mother's face, and then on the watch and chain lying just in front of Mary.

Father forgot to finish his greeting, and the hand

he was reaching out to Mary dropped down by his side.

"Hallo!   How's this?" says he.

"I have brought back Kitty's watch," says Mary.

"Brought it back!" says father.   "Back from where?"

Mary turned to me, speaking under her breath— "Kitty, if you haven't told yet, tell now! tell now!" whispered she.

But father heard, and such a look of pain came into his face as might have made anybody's heart ache.   I never can bear to think of his look that moment.

"No—no!" says he.   "Too late for that!   I'll have no more questioning of Kitty.   I never would have believed that the word of a child of mine mightn't be depended on!   Tell me yourself, Mary, and quick, for I must be off.   Where does the watch come from?"

"From Walter," she said sorrowfully.   "He has been the tempter."

"Whose tempter?"

Mary spoke clear and firm, as if she wouldn't mince matters, either for Walter's sake or for mine.

"Walter was the tempter," she said; "and Kitty has been wrong to give in to him.   Walter was in difficulties, and he got the watch from Kitty to raise money on—borrowed it, he says!   But——"

Father stood like one struck by a bolt, his head hanging down.

"And Kitty gave the watch to Russell.   Our

Kitty!" says he, in a dazed way. "Kitty! And
she making believe she didn't know aught of where
it was! Telling a pack of miserable lies! Our
Kitty! I wouldn't have believed it!" says he.

"I blame Walter most," said Mary. "He is the
oldest. If he were not so weak!"

Strange to say, even in that moment, it angered
me to hear her speak so of him. She might call
me weak, if she liked; but not Walter.

"Well, I must be off," father said, fetching a
heavy sigh. "I never could have believed it of a
child of mine. I'll see you by-and-by, Mary, and
hear all about the matter. But it's not *you* that's
to blame."

"The first I heard of it was yesterday," says
Mary, looking up into his face.

"Yes, yes—I know," says father.

Then he was gone, walking like an old man, and
never casting one glance towards me : not one.

Mother spoke next. She said in a dry sort of
tone, "It'll half kill him. He's always thought so
much of his Kitty."

And I felt as if my heart would break: as if I
couldn't bear any more: yet I wanted to hear all
that Mary had to tell. I craved to know how she'd
found out about the watch; and I was frightened
for Walter, with a fear that he might have to go
to prison for it. Being half-strangled with sobs,
I made a sort of movement like going away, not
knowing whether to go or stay; and mother said in
that same dry voice—

" Kitty, you are to stay."

" I think Kitty ought to know the whole," Mary says gently.

" I'll have everything open and above board. Kitty is to stay," said mother, looking at Mary, not at me.

Then the tale came out slowly, bit by bit, as much as Mary knew. I think I'd best tell it, partly at all events, in my own words; for there were some things I heard later, not just at that moment, and I couldn't well separate them in memory.

When Mary went home from Claxton, Walter didn't meet her at the station, as she expected; and when she got home, he wasn't there. The little maid that they kept to help, and to set Mary free for dressmaking, told her he'd had to go off somewhere, directly after dinner; she didn't know where, only he said it was business, and he'd be back as soon as possible. It was a half-holiday at the school, so he was able to get away.

Mary had all the afternoon and evening alone: for he never turned up till quite late, somewhere about eleven o'clock. When he got in he was vexed to find Mary sitting up still. " It was absurd," he said, " after her illness ! " and he would only talk of that, but wouldn't tell her where he had been. " Just a matter of business," he said. " What did women know of business ? "

If Mary had not been so worried, she must have smiled; for she had twice as good a business-head as he. But she was in no smiling mood. She knew too well that secrecy on his part meant mischief.

As Walter had told me, Mary always kept a sharp look-out over the money that came into the house, more especially school-money. She told mother and me this, telling too her reason frankly, though with shame. She seemed bent on hiding nothing. When they first went to Littleburgh, she had left things more in Walter's hands; but very soon she had found it would not do. He never could keep from spending what he had in hand; and he never cared to look forward beyond the present moment.

"Not that he means to be dishonest," she said. "Walter never means to do wrong; but he is so easily bent. There is no strength of will. Sometimes I think weakness is the worst of evils, it leads to so much wrong-doing."

Then she told us how she had set going a cash-box for every penny that wasn't strictly their own, but would have to be accounted for; and every week she went into accounts with him, and paid the right amount into this box, keeping the key herself.

Before he went back to Littleburgh, leaving her ill in our house, she made him promise to go on with the same plan. Walter gave his word easily enough; and he broke it as easily. While she was away, and he was free, he spent every penny that came to him.

Then the day was fixed for Mary's return.

Up to that moment he had not troubled himself, never looking forward; but the news of Mary's coming sent him half desperate. He hadn't the courage to face her displeasure. Before Mary he was a coward. I don't think I wonder—now! There was something in those honest eyes of hers which might well make him shrink; and she had the mastery over him too, of a strong over a weak nature. I didn't believe him to be weak then; at least, I wouldn't let myself allow that he was; but one's sight gets clearer as one goes on.

Well, as I say, Walter was in despair. There was the money short; and Mary would go into the matter straight, and every penny would have to be accounted for to her. If not to her, it would have to be accounted for to others, only a few weeks later. But Walter never looked far ahead, Mary said, speaking of this. He lived just in the present, and put off anxieties, and always expected everything to come straight somehow.

In his dread he fled away from the sight of Mary, building his hopes on poor little me, and resolving not to go home at all if I failed him. Getting hold of my watch wouldn't really help him out of his trouble, of course; but all he thought of was just being tided over the moment's pinch, and so long as he could put off the evil day he was content. Anyway, he was sure I wouldn't betray him.

I didn't fail him; more's the pity! for by giving in I was helping him along an evil road.

So he went home, telling Mary not a word; and next morning he shirked giving over the money-box to her, until he'd been to a jeweller's and had raised money on the watch, enough to pay back all that was missing; enough, too, for a good sum to be in his own pocket as well.

Mary found nothing wrong when she looked into money-matters, which was a great relief to her; and Walter was in high spirits—"particularly affectionate," she told us. And yet she couldn't help an uneasy feeling that things weren't right; and Walter would not let drop a single word about where he had been, the day she went home.

Two or three nights went by, nothing out of the way happening, and all seeming to go smooth: only she got puzzled at Walter having more money than he ought to have had. He wasn't "deep," though he was deceitful, and he'd often let slip things that he meant to keep to himself.

Mary found him buying a new tie, which he didn't need, and then some smart new studs turned up. When she asked how he'd been able to afford them, he said something about having been "careful," and next he told her the studs were "a present from a friend," only he wouldn't say what friend.

There was a good deal altogether, you see, to worry her.

On the afternoon of the day before Mary brought back the watch, the policeman called to speak to her. She knew him at once for a policeman, though he was in plain clothes. He said he went so, because he didn't wish to make a stir, nor to draw attention, but there were a few questions he must ask.

"Do you want to see my brother? He is out now," says Mary, wondering what it could all mean.

"It'll do if I can speak to you first," says the policeman.

Then he put some questions about us—how long she'd known us, when she'd left us, and so on.

Mary gave him the date of the day she was hurt, and, quite natural-like, spoke of me stopping the train with holding up mother's red shawl as a danger-signal.

"Yes, to be sure," says the policeman. "She had a reward for that too "—meaning me.

"The best reward was knowing of all the lives she'd saved," said Mary. "But the Earl of Leigh gave her a gold watch and chain too."

"And you've seen 'em, no doubt," says the policeman.

"Many times, while I was in the house," Mary answered.

"And know where they were kept," says the policeman.

"Yes; quite well," says Mary.

Then of a sudden it darted into her mind what all this meant.

"Has Kitty lost the watch?" says she.

"That's just it!" says the policeman.

"Did they send you to tell me?" says Mary.

"No; they don't know I'm come," says he.

Mary said "Ah!" to this, and a little smile came over her face. She looked up at him with that same smile——you see, we heard the story after, from him as well as her, so I've got both sides of the picture, so to speak——and she says, "You don't think I've had anything to do with that, I hope!"

"No," says he, "I don't. I'm sure you haven't."

"I didn't know of the watch being lost till this moment," says Mary.

"No," says he, "I'm sure you didn't. It isn't *you!*"

And there was something in the way he stopped a moment, and then said the "*you,*" as if to mark that though it wasn't her it was somebody. It brought up the thought of Walter with a blow. What did he mean? Mary's smile went, and she said—

"I don't understand."

"There's one or two things I don't understand neither," says the policeman. "And I've come to you to help me. Maybe you can explain 'em."

"I'll try," Mary said; and a fear crept over her mind. Was it Walter—Walter? She kept saying this to herself.

"Can you tell me where your brother was the afternoon of the day you came home?" says the policeman. He was very civil and kind all through. He couldn't have been more so, Mary said. There wasn't a rough word.

"No," Mary said; and her heart did sink, for she had suspected mischief of some sort all along.

"He wasn't here, eh?" says the policeman.

Mary never thought of such a thing as shuffling, or trying to put him off. She always was as open as the day. If I had but been the same! Mary would never say a word that wasn't true, to shelter anybody.

"No," she said, "he wasn't here! I thought he would be, and I was disappointed. He had gone off for the afternoon."

"Gone off where," says the policeman.

"I don't know where," says she.

"He didn't tell you."

"No," says she; "he only told me it was business."

"And he didn't let out he'd been to Claxton."

Mary gave a regular jump. Somehow she'd never guessed that.

"You hadn't heard it," says the policeman.

"No," says she, looking quiet still, for all she was upset. "What makes you think he went to Claxton?"

"I know he did. He was seen," says the policeman.

"What time?" Mary asked.

"Just before dark, in a lane near the line."

"Near the station?" says Mary; and he nodded.

"I can't think why he shouldn't have told me," says Mary, thinking out aloud.

"Something he wanted to hide, that's plain," says the policeman.

Mary went as white as a sheet.

"O no, not Walter!   O no, not that!" she cried, and a big sob came from her heart.   "He never would!   He never could!   How dare you say such a thing of my Walter?"

The policeman wasn't vexed.   "I didn't say it," he answered.   "Maybe I didn't think it either."

"But you said——" and Mary stopped.

"No," says he, "I didn't say that.   If I thought anybody had gone and stolen the watch, my duty 'ud be plain.   I shouldn't need to stand talking here."

Mary sat down and waited, not speaking a word; and he went on—

"I don't say it's that.   But I've a notion there's something between Mr. Phrynne's daughter and your brother.   I've a notion they both know where the watch and chain are."

"Kitty!" says Mary.

"That's it," says he, grave-like.   "Easy to see she wasn't speaking truth to her father nor me; and folks say she was wonderful taken with him. Now if so be she gave him the watch, he didn't steal it, and yet maybe he's got it!   More than that I don't say—only I've got to find out where the watch is; and the quieter it's done, the better pleased Mr. Phrynne 'll be."

Well, that wasn't all that passed, but by this time Mary pretty well understood how things were.

L

The worst of the matter was that she couldn't help fearing the policeman was in the right. Putting two and two together, it seemed likely.

You see, she'd no manner of security about Walter. She might cry out in hot defence of him: "He never would! He never could!" but to say the same words in quiet certainty was another matter.

After a while it was settled that Mary should have a talk with her brother the same evening, and the policeman would call again later. It showed his trust in Mary, that he was willing to wait. She told him she knew she had more power over Walter than anybody else; and she thought she could bring him to confess. She promised for Walter that he should be there, when the policeman called.

"Well, I'll risk it," said he at last. "I'll risk it. Don't seem to me there's been downright dishonesty: though there's been a lot of deceiving. Anyhow, I've got to get to the bottom of the matter. And the quieter it's done the better; only mind you, Mr. Phrynne is bent on getting back the watch."

Then the policeman went away, and Mary knelt down just where she was, all alone, to pray to be made to say the right words. It must have been a sorrowful hour that she passed, waiting for her brother; only she had the comfort of praying.

Walter had his tea when he came back, and he

seemed uncommon lively, as he'd been the past few days. Mary couldn't eat nor talk through the meal, but Walter did plenty of both.

"What's the matter?" says he at last. "You look dumpish."

Mary had not made up her mind when nor how to speak; but in a moment she resolved not to put it off.

"Walter!" says she, looking at him, "why didn't you tell me you had been to Claxton the day I came home?"

Walter went as red as fire.

"So Kitty's let that out, has she?" said he. "The little ass!"

Well, you can suppose I didn't like to be called an "ass," even by Walter. Mary told it out quietly, telling the story.

She did not at once say that he was mistaken.

"Why should Kitty keep your going there a secret?" said she.

"Why, of course—because—oh, only because—well, of course she needn't!" said he, floundering.

"Wouldn't it be natural she should speak after she'd seen you?" says Mary.

"Natural!" says he; and he muttered again, "The little ass!"

"Did you see Kitty alone, or all of them together?" Mary asked.

"Only Kitty!" says he sulkily. "It wasn't anybody else's concern."

"Then that was the business you went after,"

Mary said. "I don't see why you should make such a mystery of it," says she.

Walter wouldn't answer.

"However, you needn't blame Kitty, for it was not Kitty who told me," Mary went on.

"Not Kitty!" says he, staring.

"No," said she, "Kitty never said a word—more's the pity."

"Then what did you mean by telling me she did?" said he.

"I didn't tell you so, Walter. It was you accused Kitty, not I," says Mary. "I heard in another way. It has made me very unhappy," says she.

"Rubbish," says he. "I'm not bound to tell everything to everybody."

"No," said she. "But you are bound not to run after Kitty without her parents' consent—not to see her in secret—and not—— "

Mary couldn't go on.

"Well! anything else?" says he gloomily. "I suppose you'll go and make a fine tale of all this to the Phrynnes."

"It's too much of a tale already," says she. "I've no need to make any more of it." And then she said, "Walter, how could you?"

"How could I what? See Kitty! Stuff and nonsense!" said he. "If I did have a word with her, what's the harm? 'All's fair in love and war!'" says he, and he tried to laugh.

"Wrong-doing is never fair," Mary told him.

And she said, "If you loved Kitty, you could not wish to make her deceitful."

"Well, you needn't bother," said he.

"And that is not all," Mary went on. "How could you——"

"How could I what?" said he, very short. "Tell Kitty she had a pretty face?"

"How could you rob her of her watch?" Mary said.

He was taken by surprise, and Mary's words struck home at last. He turned as white as paste, and a frightened look came into his face. If she'd asked him whether he'd done it, he'd have said, "No;" but she didn't ask him that, and no doubt he felt sure she knew a deal more than she did know.

"Why—why—why—" says he, stammering, "I declare, Mary, that's a—a nice thing to accuse a chap of! 'Rob,' indeed! When she gave it me!" says he.

"Did Kitty make a present to you of her watch and chain?" Mary asked.

When Mary came to this part in her story, I could understand what Walter had meant by calling Mary stern. As she said the words, telling mother all about it, she did look stern.

"Well, not exactly a—present, perhaps," says he, stumbling over his words. "But she gave them over to me. I do assure you she did, Mary," says he, as if it was an excuse for himself.

"Gave them over to you—what for?" says Mary.

Walter wouldn't tell at first, and then he shuffled. I'd given them over to him to do what he liked with them—at least, it wasn't exactly a present, but a loan—at least, it was just to tide him over a difficulty, when he was hard-pressed—at least——

Mary got out of patience with him, I suppose, for she cut sharp into his talk. "At least, you wheedled poor little Kitty out of them!" says she.

Mother hadn't looked at me once for ever so long, and I don't think Mary had either. I stood leaning against the dresser still, feeling like one stupefied, yet able to take in every word that Mary said, so that I never could forget any of it again. I had stopped crying. I was listening too hard to leave any time or power for tears.

I heard a sort of catch in my own breath, when Mary got so far; and Mary must have heard it too, for she turned round towards me, and said—

"Kitty, did you *give* the watch and chain to Walter?"

I was startled by the sudden question, and I said, "O no!"—not stopping to think.

"Then you lent them to him! But what for?" said she.

"He—asked me!" I said.

"Come here, Kitty," said she, and I came close. Mary took my hand in a grave sort of way, not stern now.

"But if you lent him the watch and chain, you did not mean him to sell them?"

I was startled again into saying "O no!"

"No; so I supposed. He talked to you about loans, and raising money, and passing difficulties—did he not?"

It was so exactly what he had done, that I hung my head.

"Poor silly child!" Mary said.

I couldn't bear to have them both looking at me, and I dropped down on the floor, hiding my face in Mary's dress. Somehow her touch was a comfort, even while it made me more ashamed.

"Then he sold the watch," mother said, in a hard voice.

"Yes," Mary told us. He had sold the watch and chain—sold them, after all his promises to me! To be sure, he had spoken to the jeweller of "pressing difficulties," and of hoping to buy them back in the course of a few weeks; but anybody might know what that was worth.

Mary had had hard work to get at the truth of the matter. Walter had shuffled and doubled, and tried every means in his power to put her off with half-answers. But she had refused to be put off.

"What on earth made the girl tell of me?" Walter burst forth angrily at last.

Then Mary explained how things had oozed out; and when Walter heard of the policeman's call, he turned yellow-white again, and was like a terrified child.

"I can't see the man, Mary! I can't see the man!" says he, shaking with fright. "You'll see him, there's a dear! I'm going to bed," says he.

But Mary wouldn't let him off.   She had given her word to the policeman, she said.

Walter gave in then, and made a clean breast of everything from first to last—all about how he'd got into difficulties, and how he'd used all the money he could lay hands on, and how he'd begged the watch and chain from me for just a few days, meaning to take them to a pawnbroker's, and how the temptation had come over him to sell them outright, and how of course he was very miserable, and never, never, would do anything of the sort again.

But the miserableness wasn't repentance!   Walter minded being found out—not being in the wrong!

The policeman was so far satisfied with what he heard, that he left it in Mary's hands to get back the watch and chain from the jeweller's in the morning: which she was happily able to do, since he had not sold it.   I did not hear till long after that Mary had to pay a good deal over what Walter had received for it.   Thanks to his extravagance, the only way in which she could do this was by parting with the two or three trinkets of value which had come to her from her mother.

" Kitty, it has been a foolish business—worse than foolish," Mary said, when her story was ended.

And that was true enough.   It did look very foolish, very wrong.   I felt as miserable as Walter could have felt: partly knowing how I'd been in the wrong: partly a sort of disappointment in him.

I did think, after I'd done and borne so much, he needn't have been so ready to say hard words of me. I'm almost afraid that was the uppermost thought with me, as I sat on the floor, hiding my face in Mary's dress; and yet there was real sorrow below.

"You'll stay here to-night," mother said to Mary. She spoke still in a hard sort of voice, as if she couldn't trust herself.

"O no—only to dinner. I must go home early," Mary said.

Mother didn't press for more. She seemed too down-hearted to care.

"Kitty, you'd best be about your work. You've sat there long enough," says she.

It was the first time in all my life mother had ever spoken to me in that tone—almost as if I was a stranger. Mother wasn't given to showing anger in her manner, as I've said earlier. But then she'd never before found me out in a course of deceit, and she was bitterly disappointed in her Kitty. She and father too—ah, poor father! If I had but been able to look forward, and to see what was coming!

When mother spoke, I got up, and stood still in a dazed way. Mary said, almost whispering—

"Haven't you a word to say to your mother, Kitty?"

But mother broke in, sharp and short—

"No, Mary, I won't have Kitty prompted," said she. "If Kitty don't know what she ought to do,

she needn't do it! Saying at somebody's bidding
don't mean much. And I don't know either as
Kitty's words 'll be worth anything to me ever
again," says she. "I did think I could trust her;
and I can't."

"Kitty will win her way back to your trust,"
says Mary.

"Maybe," mother said. "It'll take a lot of
winning, though. I wasn't easy persuaded that she
could deceive me—not even when the policeman
said so, for I thought it was a mistake. And I
shan't be easy persuaded to trust her again."

"But you love her still," pleaded Mary. "A
mother always loves her child. You'll help her to
get back into the right path." And then Mary
turned to me again, and said, "Kitty!"—pleading-
like.

I knew she meant I ought to beg mother's
pardon; and it's hard to tell now why I didn't.
Mother's manner kept me off, partly, and I felt
stupefied, and the real pain at my heart was
about Walter, not so much yet about mother and
father.

"You can go and finish the bedrooms," mother
said to me. "And take that watch away; I don't
want to see it again," says she.

But I wouldn't touch the watch; and Mary
took it up.

"No," said she; "I think *you* had better keep
the watch for a time, Mrs. Phrynne, until Kitty
has proved herself trustworthy."

Mother let Mary put it into her hands ; and then
I ran off.

Some days do seem long compared to others ;
and that was one of the longest I've ever known.
The minutes crawled so, I didn't know how to get
through them.

I made the work upstairs last as long as I could,
and then I sat mending, not speaking a word to
anybody. It is strange now to remember how
silent I was ; and I do remember it, and how when
Mary spoke to me I hardly answered ; yet at the
time I didn't feel silent. My thoughts were so busy,
going round and round in a whirl.

Walter—Walter—Walter—just filled my mind.
I felt as if a great wall had grown up between him
and me ; and I longed to get beyond the wall. I
couldn't respect him for the way he had gone on,
and I was angry with the way he had spoken of
me, and yet I couldn't bear to think that most
likely he thought I had broken my promise and
had betrayed him. Somehow that weighed upon
me more than anything. I did long to make it all
clear to him, even if he and I were never to meet
again after ; and the thought of never meeting made
my heart come into my throat, as it were.

One moment I was vexed with him, and felt how
meanly and unworthily he had acted. Then the
very next moment I'd see his face, as he had looked
when he called me "his little Kitty," and I seemed
ready to cry out with longing to have him near me
again—even while in my conscience I couldn't but

condemn his deceit and cowardice. Not that I let
myself use any such words about him at that time.
I only felt : I didn't say.

A little while before dinner, father came in. I
had gone upstairs again, for I was so restless I
couldn't keep still ; and I saw him from my window.
I knew he and Mary would have a talk together
about me ; and I didn't go down, but left mother
to get the dinner. Mother never called me, as
she'd have done usually. And when I went down,
father scarce looked at me. That did pierce deep,
for I was used to such tenderness. It was as
much as I could do to bear the change in him.

I don't know much of what was said by anybody
at dinner. I only know how sad and down-hearted
father seemed, and how Mary looked as if she did
feel for him so.

But he never said a word to me all dinner-time.
For I hadn't so much as told him nor mother yet
that I was sorry for all I'd done.

Father went off again the moment he had finished ; and mother was called out to speak to somebody in the kitchen. That left Mary and me alone.

I thought in a moment that she would begin by
finding fault with her brother, and that I would
not agree.

But her first words were not what I expected ;
they took me altogether by surprise.

"Kitty," says she, "what am I to say to Walter
from you ?"

CHAPTER IX.

THEN——

I WAS so taken aback with the question, I sat and stared at Mary. For it was about the last thing in the world I looked for, that she should offer to take a message from me to her brother.

"Am I to say—nothing?" she asked.

It rushed over me then how I'd been longing all the morning to let him know that I had kept my promise. And I never waited to think if that was the sort of message Mary had in her mind.

"Yes, please," I said, trembling. "Please tell Mr. Russell it wasn't my fault."

I don't think I shall soon forget the astonished look that came over Mary's face. She had got something she didn't expect; that was clear.

"What wasn't your fault?" said she.

"About—about its getting known," I whispered, twisting a corner of the tablecloth into a little rope, and dreadfully afraid mother would come back before I could explain. "I'm afraid he'll think it was me, and indeed it wasn't. I never let out a word."

"Is that all you care for, Kitty?" said she, in a sad tone.

"No," I said, and I found it hard to speak. "No, I do care, and I am sorry. It's been wrong, I know. Only—I can't bear him to think——"

"Walter's thinking either way is worth very little, poor weak boy that he is," said she. "Kitty, have you never thought how all this has been in the sight of God? '

I said "Yes," very low; and it was true, for I had not forgotten that. Only it had weighed second with me, not first; and so Mary understood.

"Perhaps you have thought in a passing way, but you have not cared," said she. "At least, not much. Not half so much as you have cared about what people may say of you."

If she had said "Walter" instead of "people," she would have been in the right.

"I don't know," was all I could answer.

After a minute, she began again.

"What am I to say to Walter about your watch?"

I began to see what sort of a message Mary had meant, and I didn't speak.

"Mind, Kitty," said she, "your words may have power one way or another—for good or for evil. I don't say they will have, for I'm not sure whether you have any power at all over Walter; but they may. Most people have some sort of power over pretty nearly every one else. Walter has robbed you. What am I to say?"

"Oh, not robbed," I said.

"He has *robbed* you," she said again firmly. "It

is no thanks to Walter that you have the watch again. He has acted with downright dishonesty, and nothing less. He got the watch from you on false pretences—yes, false!" she repeated, as I whispered "O no!" again. "He is my own brother, but that is no reason for explaining away the sin. Because I love him, I am only the more grieved. Loving him can't make me love evil. I want you to look the truth in the face; not to mince matters. No good is ever gained by saying that black is white. Walter robbed you of your watch, under pretence of borrowing it."

Yes, she was stern; she could be almost hard. At least, I tried to think so, trying still to defend Walter in my heart.

"But he didn't mean——" I murmured.

"Didn't mean to rob you! My dear, he meant to get a certain amount of money somehow; he cared very little how. What *you* might lose or suffer was quite a small matter. Kitty,—if I could open your eyes to understand him!"

I had a sort of side-peep of mother putting her head round the door, and going away again. It flurried me so, I didn't know what to say. And I was angry with Mary too. Why must she make the very worst of everything to do with Walter?

"He meant to bring it back to me," I said.

"To bring back the watch! After he had sold it!"

"Perhaps he didn't really quite sell it," I whispered.

"He sold it, quite and really," says she.   "How could he sell it only half? You are fighting against truth, trying to believe in him still," says she.   "Will anything persuade you, short of coming to the jeweller's with me?"

I said "O no!" to that.

"No, you don't want to go—is that it? Then will you take my word? He sold the watch and chain for more money than he was in need of, and spent a lot in useless nothings. That is Walter all over! Do you think I don't know him now, after all these years?"

I didn't make any answer.

"It is the old story," says she sorrowfully; "only worse. And I did hope things were going to be better. Kitty, you have been helping him along the downward path, deeper into evil. If you really cared for him, you could not have done so."

"O no!" I said again.   "Not——"

"Helping him downward into evil," said she. "Nothing less! Helping him farther along the road of deceit and dishonesty, and letting him teach you to deceive. If only you had stood firm when he tempted you, there'd have been sin spared on both sides. It is one of the saddest tales I have ever heard," said she.   "One of the saddest, after the training you have had—and with such a father and mother! Perhaps you fancy you gave in because you like Walter. He's nice-looking, and he can say pretty things to girls. But it's a poor sort of 'liking' for a person, that can make you help forward the evil in him. And I, his sister, don't thank you for the harm you have done. Some day you will repent it too."

Then she stopped, as if to give me time to speak; and I said nothing. I was angry still, and shamed and unhappy; and if I might not defend Walter, I would not answer at all. So after a minute she said softly—

" Good-bye, Kitty. I shall pray for you."

Then she went away out of the room, leaving me alone ; and I didn't follow nor see her again, for she went by the train that passed in a quarter of an hour.

Mother brought her work in soon, and sat down at the table. We had a lot of mending to get through, and I knew it had to be done. I felt half wild, as the minutes dragged on, and the clock ticked, and not a word was said. It seemed to my fancy as if mother wouldn't trust me, and was keeping guard. I longed to get away somewhere alone, for a good cry; yet I didn't dare to stir.

I can remember how mother looked, sitting still sideways towards me, her fingers stitching on and on steady as a machine, and her eyes never lifting themselves. She had such a quietness in her face, as if she was waiting and expecting something.

It must have been near two hours that we kept like that, both of us working, and not saying a word. But at last I couldn't bear myself any longer. I was aching all over, and restlessness

M

wouldn't be held down. I dropped the table-cloth I was mending, and leant back in my chair.

Mother looked up then slowly, and fixed her eyes on me, like one coming out of a dream. She didn't ask if I was poorly, nor say I'd better go for a run, as was her way commonly; but she seemed to be trying to find out something; and all at once she said—

"Kitty, have you promised Mr. Russell to be his wife some day?"

"No, mother," I said, getting as red as fire.

"He has asked you, I suppose?" said she.

"No, mother," I said.

Mother gazed at me still, and sighed. "It's not much use putting questions," said she. "How am I to know it's truth you tell me?"

"Oh, but——" I said. "I wouldn't——"

"You wouldn't tell more fibs than happens to be convenient," said she; and I hadn't often heard harder words from mother. "No, I dare say not," says she. "But you see I mightn't know when it *was* convenient."

"Mother, I wish you wouldn't talk so," I said, feeling wretched.

"I dare say," says she. "And I wish I had a child again that I could believe in. I could have stood anything better than that—anything, I do think," said she. "It's like losing my Kitty that I've always trusted, and having somebody else instead."

"I'll never tell a story again," I said earnestly. "Never! I won't really."

" No," said she, sorrowful-like. " You don't mean to—maybe."

And I saw she hadn't a grain of confidence in me. Was it any wonder?

" You say Mr. Russell never asked you to marry him. Then what did go on between you two?" said she. " If you are minded to begin speaking the truth, tell me all out plain now."

She looked so anxious, leaving her work, and waiting to hear. And I was all in confusion, not knowing what I might or mightn't say. Perhaps I ought rather to put it, that I was puzzled between my wish to please mother and not to say a word that Mr. Russell could mind.

" He was—so good to me," I whispered.

" How?" said she.

" He was—kind," I said.

" That won't do, Kitty. I must hear more, if I hear anything," said she. " Did he ever ask you to marry him?"

" No," I said; and that was true. " He only——"

" Well? He only—what?" said she.

" He only seemed—to think—to think—I liked him," said I, stumbling.

" That's truth, I don't doubt," said she; and she repeated the words: " Only seemed to think you liked him! I'd like to have seen the man, when *I* was a girl, who'd have dared to seem to think I liked him, before he'd made it pretty plain how much he liked me! But I don't know what's

come over the girls nowadays.   They haven't a
scrap of self-respect."

"O but, mother, he did seem——" I began,
and stopped.

"Did seem what?" says she.   "Did seem to
think he liked you too?   Is that all?"

I wouldn't speak, for I remembered how I'd
promised not to tell.

"There's a deal of 'seeming,'" said she.   "Seeming this and seeming that!   A few honest-spoken
words would be worth a lot more than all the
seeming.   Kitty, did he ever tell you he loved
you?"

"Not—not exactly," I whispered.

"No, not exactly, I'll be bound," says she.   "Just
enough to win a silly girl's heart, and just little
enough to leave himself free!   I know the ways of
that sort."

And wasn't it true?

"But I'm sure he did mean——" I began, and
stopped again.

"Did mean what?" said she.

"He did call me 'his own little Kitty,'" I whispered, in a shamefaced way.   Mother's questioning
put my promise out of my head again.   I was
getting to feel all in a whirl.

"And you let him!" said she.

I shan't soon forget the quiet tone, and the con-
tempt of it.

"You let him call you *that*, before even he'd
asked if you would marry him!" says mother.

"I thought—he seemed——" I whispered.

"There you are again, with your thinking and seeming," said she. "Nothing open nor above-board."

"He did say—something," I muttered. "He did say something—something about—he hoped some day—and if he was to ask me——"

"If he was to ask you what?" says she.

But I didn't go on.

"If he was to ask you to marry him?" says she. "But he didn't ask you! That's the last thing you said. Whichever am I to believe?"

"He didn't ask me to marry him—really—truly—mother," I answered. "He only said something about—he'd like some day—and—and if he was to ask me—would I——"

And then I fell into a fright.

"O I oughtn't to have said so much. I promised him I wouldn't."

"That's a nice state of things," says she. "A man making you an offer, and you not to tell your own mother!"

"Only not just yet," I pleaded. "And it wasn't—that—it wasn't truly, mother. He didn't ask—that! He only said—if he *was* to ask—by-and-by——"

"Piece of impertinence!" said she.

"Mother! you don't understand, and I can't make you," I said.

"I understand part," says she; "and that is, he took precious good care to keep himself free. 'If he was to ask you,' indeed! Impertinence!" says she again, and I don't know as I'd ever before seen mother so hot. " Catch a man in my young days," says she, " asking if I'd hold myself ready to say ' yes,' the moment he chose to ask me—if so be he ever did ask I I'm in doubt whether to be most amazed at him or at you, Kitty," says she.

"I oughtn't to have told; I promised him I wouldn't. Mother I don't tell father," I begged.

She sat looking at me in a sort of wonder.

"Asking me not to tell father!" says she. " Kitty, are you crazy? or d'you suppose I'm crazy?"

Then, between one worry and another, and having had so much on my mind, I turned queer and ill again, worse than the day before. Mother helped me upstairs, and made me lie down on my bed. She was kind as could be, and did all I needed; only there wasn't the tenderness I was used to, and I did miss it.

I couldn't go downstairs again that afternoon nor evening. I couldn't, partly because I felt bad, and partly because I dreaded what father would say. Mother let me do as I wished. She didn't press me either way. And father never came to my room at all. It was the first time I could re-member father not coming to see how I was, when I had not been well.

Next morning I had breakfast in bed, for I couldn't sleep much; and I didn't hurry going down after, so father was off first.

Half-way through the morning Mr. Armstrong

came in. He had heard from father something of
what had happened, and he said he had called to
ask me all about it. Mother just said, " Yes, thank
you, sir. Kitty 'll take you into the parlour."

I didn't like that, but I had to go. Mr. Armstrong was very gentle, and never spoke hard
words; but all the same—perhaps all the more
because of the gentleness—I cared a deal more for
what he said than for most people.

He had been a kind friend to me all my life, and
he had prepared me for Confirmation only two years
sooner. Somehow when he sat down near me, I
couldn't help thinking of the time I had seen him
alone just before my Confirmation, and how he had
spoken of the life I was to lead as a "servant of
Jesus Christ;" and how I was to obey Him, and
love Him, and set myself to please Him in everything I did. I had little thought then how soon I
was to be led into a crooked path of deceit. It
was curious the remembrance of that time coming
just then into my head. I expected Mr. Armstrong
to begin asking me a lot of questions, and I was
determined I wouldn't let out more than I could
help about Walter Russell. But instead of beginning with questions, Mr. Armstrong kept silence
a minute, as if he wanted to give me time. And
then he said—

" 'My duty towards my neighbour is—to be true
and just in all my dealings—to keep my tongue
from lying!'"

I knew those words well enough, of course.

Mother had taught me the Catechism through and through from almost my babyhood, and I knew my way about in it blindfold, if one may speak so. As I say, I was thinking already of my Confirmation, and all the teaching I'd had before; and these words seemed to bring back a great wave-like of the feelings I'd had then, and how I had longed and resolved always to do right and to please God.

"I think you have forgotten that lately, Kitty," says Mr. Armstrong.

I whispered a "Yes."

"Forgotten everything except just having your own will," says he. "Nothing surer to land one in evil than putting *first* how to please self. If the thought of pleasing God comes second, it soon ends by being nowhere."

And I said "Yes" again, for I knew it was true.

He spoke most beautiful to me after that, not putting a great many questions, but talking in a gentle way, like a father might talk. He said how grieved and disappointed my father and mother were, and how good they'd always been to me, and how sad it was I should grieve them. That made my tears come fast, and he stopped and looked at me.

"No," said he. "She is not hardened. It isn't hardness." And then he says, "Kitty," says he, "you want to get back into the right road, don't you? I know you do," says he.

"Yes," I whispered.

"And you are sorry too," says he.

I said "Yes" again.

"And you'll tell your father and mother so, Kitty?"

"Yes," I sobbed; "only——"

"But there mustn't be any 'only,'". says he. "You've got to give up your own way, and be ready to have God's way—and that means submitting to your parents," says he. "No good to talk of being sorry without submitting too. You must tell your father and mother you won't go against them, nor hide anything again. Repentance means turning from evil. It doesn't mean just saying you're sorry, and going on still in the same way."

I knew this; but still the thought of Walter came up.

Mr. Armstrong went on next to speak of the sin of my conduct towards God. He spoke of the dreadful nature of untruth, and how God looked upon falsehood. He told me of the danger of it, and how if I got entangled in paths of deceit, I should be dragged down and down, nobody could tell how low. Then he reminded me of my Confirmation, and how I had solemnly promised to serve Christ the Lord.

"But this isn't serving Christ," he said sadly. "This has been serving the evil one." And he said how I must have grieved the gentle Spirit of God by what I'd done, till I felt as if my heart would break with listening to him.

"Kitty, don't you be half and half now," said

he; "don't let it be a sham repentance. Be real and thorough, whatever else you are. Make up your mind to give up all, to let everything go, rather than grieve the Holy Spirit any more. Don't cling to your own way. It isn't worth while! The things you have cared for lately are not worth having when you get them. The cost is too great. It is *not worth while*, Kitty," says he again, and I couldn't afterward forget the tone of those words. "There's so much to lose on the one side, and so little to gain on the other."

But the bonds were holding me yet. While I listened I was touched; still I felt that, if the choice was mine, I couldn't choose to give up Mr. Russell. Mr. Armstrong's words pulled hard; and in the midst of them came a great pull the other way—a sudden thought of Walter's voice calling me "his own little Kitty." And I was dragged in half between them—poor silly child that I was—turning from gold to hanker after common dust!

I did promise faithfully to beg father's pardon next time I saw him; but Mr. Armstrong couldn't get me to say all he wanted.

The rest of the morning I was in a quake, thinking what I had said I would do, and so restless I didn't know how to settle to work.

Mother left me pretty much to myself: only I always felt she had her eye upon me, as if I wasn't to be trusted out of sight.

Father came in at dinner-time, and I was

tongue-tied, as if I couldn't speak a word. Which was nonsense, for of course I could speak. It was want of will, not want of power, that held me back. And I had not prayed for help—at least, not freely and fully. I had the feeling still that I couldn't give up Walter.

Dinner was another silent meal. Father helped me, but he didn't talk, nor did mother. He looked so sad and downhearted, and once or twice I heard him give a great sigh.

Well, at last he got up to go, and a sort of desperate feeling came over me, that now was the turning-point, and that if I didn't speak then perhaps I never should. Besides, if I didn't keep my promise to Mr. Armstrong, nobody would ever believe me again. And with all this I felt too, so strangely, that I couldn't make myself, but God could make me; and I think I cried out in my heart for help.

Oh me! to think what I should have felt, after, if I hadn't said a word!

"Father!" I whispered, in a shaky sort of voice.

He was near the door, but he heard me, and he turned round, straight.

I've often thought since how much that one word means, and how if we're sad or downhearted, or in trouble, or in temptation, it's often enough to cry out, or even just to whisper—"FATHER!" For that means everything, and the answer is sure.

I didn't say more. I was half choked, and couldn't. And perhaps there was no need.

He seemed to understand in a moment all I meant to say. Quick as possible he came back to where I sat, and took me in his arms, and held me tight—oh, so tight—like as if he was taking me into his heart. And the tears ran down his cheeks, dropping on my face.

"Kitty, you'll never do it again—never again!" says he hoarsely.

"No, no, I won't," I sobbed.

"And you're—sorry?" says he.

"O father, I'm *so* sorry," I got out, clinging to him.

I heard him mutter, "Thank God!" and then he broke down, and sobbed too.

"There, that won't do," says he, trying hard to get over it. "I must be off to—to the station," says he, while there was another great heave of his chest, which I felt all through me. "Kitty, say that once again; say you'll never—never——"

"O no—never!" I sobbed.

Then he put me from him, and started to go; and he came back, unexpected, from the door, to catch me in his arms again, and hold me tight to him—a thing he wasn't given to doing commonly.

After that he was gone; and I couldn't so much as look at mother. I just rushed away up to my room, and cried there, fit to break my heart.

For I knew it meant giving up Walter Russell. I knew father wouldn't allow anything between him and me, after the way he had acted. I knew I oughtn't so much as to wish for it—and yet I did wish. Now and again the wish rolled up in a great wave, that seemed like to swamp everything else; and then Mr. Armstrong's words would come, —"Not worth while! not worth while! So much to gain, so little to lose!" And I did pray to be kept straight, and not allowed to go back.

It must have been a good two hours I was upstairs alone, mother never coming to interrupt me. Perhaps it's well she didn't. I was learning something, alone there with my own thoughts and with God—something maybe that had to be learnt to prepare me for the sorrow that lay ahead.

When at last I went down, it was with red eyes and changed feelings. Mother looked up at me from her work, and I saw a difference in the look, more like I was used to.

I wanted to tell her too that I was sorry, and meant to do rightly; but when I reached her side, I couldn't speak, I could only cry.

"Yes, I understand," says she, in her quiet fashion; "I understand, Kitty."

But she didn't take me straight into her arms and to her heart, like father. Mother was so unlike to father. I knew it would be a good while before she'd feel for me as she was used to feel, or give me the old trust. And I knew that would be my punishment.

"It's not good for you to cry so much," says she. "Come a turn in the garden with me. That'll make you feel better."

Mother took up her red shawl, and we went out

together. The fresh air always did me good, and I knew mother was showing forgiveness too in her own way. We didn't say anything, but went along the path on the embankment to the end.

"This is where you were when you saw the truck that day," said she.

It wasn't the spot where I stood when I saw the truck first, but I didn't see any need to contradict.

"I'm always thankful you had the sense to do your duty," says she. "But I'm none too sure it was good for you—all the fuss that was made about it."

"No, mother," I said.

"I don't hold with that sort of fuss," says she.

Then, after standing a minute, and looking at nothing particular, mother said—

"It isn't my way to make a lot of talk about what's done, and can't be undone. But I've one thing to say."

"Yes, mother," says I, meek enough; and I knew what was coming.

"About that young Russell," says she.

"Yes, mother."

"Mind, Kitty—it's all over between you and him. If there ever has been anything, which I've my doubts upon," says she, "it's over now."

I didn't speak a word, for I was that choked, I couldn't.

"He's shown himself a liar and a cheat. I'd sooner see you in your grave, Kitty, than give

you over to him. Mind, I say it, and I mean it,"
says she.

And then she touched my hand in a kind-like
way, and said—

"It won't be long. You'll soon leave caring.
There can't be love without there's respect."

"I *do* love him," I sobbed. "And oh—I don't
know how to bear it!"

"Catch me, when I was a girl, saying I loved
a man before he'd said he loved me!" I heard
mother mutter to herself. "Whatever has come
over the girls nowadays! Not a scrap of proper
self-respect."

But she touched my hand again, and patted it.

"Come! you've got to be brave," says she. "I
wouldn't give in too easy."

"I do mean—to try," I managed to say.

"Yes, I'm sure you do," says she. And she
walked me back along the path, and then again
to the end, and back a second time.

How quiet and natural everything did seem!
Looking back to that hour, it is wonderful to me to
think of us two, loitering out to and fro, getting the
fresh air, and having our talk, with never so much
as a fancy of what was just about to happen.

Isn't that how we go through life: step by step
onward, none of us able ever to see where the next
step will land us? If it wasn't for the thought of
a Father's Hand over all, managing and arranging for
us, we should have good reason to be frightened.

Sometimes one does get frightened trying to peer

ahead. But it was not so with me just then.
Nothing was farther from my mind than the fear of
any fresh trouble. It seemed to me I had enough
to bear.

I was stepping along slowly beside mother,
gazing down on the ground, when suddenly mother
stopped short, and I heard such a strange sound
from her! It was as if she wanted to speak,
and couldn't. I looked up quick, thinking she must
be taken ill; and she was the most extraordinary
colour, not white, nor grey, but a mixture of both,
and her lips parted and stiff.

"Mother!" I began, in a frightened way; and it
flashed over me how if she was going to die it would
be my fault for grieving her so. But before I could
say another word, the sound came again; and I saw
her eyes staring, and her hand pointing at something
—something down below, on the line, nearer the
station.

Quick as lightning I turned my eyes down there,
and saw the whole!

Folks say moments are all of the same length.
I don't know. It don't seem to me they can be.
For that next moment was the longest I ever lived
through in my life. It stretched out and out in
an awful way; and yet it *couldn't* have been more
than a moment. If it had been, things would
have ended different. There would have been time,
which there wasn't.

There's a danger to men always, near and about the
line, which outside folks don't understand. They're

always within hearing of trains, and they get so used to the sound that at last they don't hear it, hardly. If they are not on the watch, a train might rush by within a few yards, and they wouldn't notice the stir. It's natural, seeing we get used to pretty near everything which we have always in everyday life; but it means danger. Many a poor fellow has been maimed, or even killed, just through being overmuch accustomed to the station sounds, and so not hearing the train that was bearing down upon him.

Father was careful commonly, knowing the danger, which he'd sometimes spoken about. But it's hard for a man to be always on the alert, and that day in particular—ah me!—he had his mind full of something else.

When I looked, I saw all in an instant. I saw, too, that there was nothing for me to do.

A train was coming along the curve from behind us towards the station——one of the fast trains that didn't stop, but ran through.

Father was down on the line, just outside the station, calling out something to a man at a little distance from him, on the other side. Father's back was turned to us; and just before I saw him, he had stepped unthinkingly back upon the rails, along which the train was coming.

He only had to step forward again, and he was all right. But that was just what he didn't think of doing.

I knew in one glance that father didn't see or

hear.   I saw the man father was speaking to wave his arms, and shout a warning, but father never took in what he meant.   I noticed even that the driver and the stoker of the coming engine were doing their best, calling out, and sounding the whistle.   But no use.   It was all part of what father was always hearing.   His mind was off, somewhere else.

There wasn't time to stop the train before it must reach him.   I knew that.   And I knew I could still less get to him ; yet I think I screamed, and ran forward.   But the rush of the train which he did not notice drowned all else.

Mother never stirred, and not another sound came from her.

Then——

CHAPTER X.

SHARP AND SUDDEN.

YES; they did their best to stop in time. But it was no use; for the brakes of those days were slow-acting; and before the train could do more than begin to slacken, all was over.

The buffer caught him first, and swept him along; and then he was among the cruel wheels; and what they left of him was no longer—father!

It couldn't have been more than a moment's shock of pain. Not to him, I mean! But oh, the shock and pain to us who loved him!

He was so ready to go. He had loved and lived for his Master for many a year. Not that he was ever much of a talker about religion; but he lived it, which is worth a deal more. I know he was readier for death than we were for the sorrow of losing him.

Sunday after Sunday we pray in Church against sudden death. "From sudden death, good Lord, deliver us!" But doesn't sudden death mean death unprepared for? I don't think death can ever be "sudden" in the real sense of the word to those who are ready and waiting. I think the stroke of the buffer, which startled and swept him away, was nothing more nor less to father than just the voice of his Master bidding him " Come Home!" One moment of start and fright, maybe; and then—nothing but joy.

When the train came to a stop, a little way farther on, after the cruel deed was done—not that anybody could be blamed!—several gentlemen got out; and the driver of the engine sat down on the ground, and hid his face, and cried like a child at the awfulness of what had happened. But, poor fellow, nobody could find fault with him!

Mother saw the whole from first to last. She never took her eyes away; and when the mangled body was tossed out by the wheels upon the six-foot way, she went swiftly down, never faltering, and knelt beside it, and wouldn't be torn away till the doctor came and told her all was over—as she might have seen. But they said she didn't seem to see. Her eyes were fixed, and she never spoke a word, nor shed a tear.

I saw nothing more after the moment that the buffer struck father. It must have been a long faint. When I struggled back to sense, with a strange dreadful feeling that some sort of thunderbolt had fallen on us, Mr. Baitson and Lady Arthur and Mrs. Hammond were all standing over me, and I was down on the floor in our kitchen.

" Poor things! How terrible for them!" I heard Lady Arthur say.

" And they seeing it all! Why, it's enough to

kill 'em—more than enough," Mrs. Hammond said,
in the brisk sort of way she had.

"Hush!" Mr. Baitson said, quite low.

And I opened my eyes, and looked at them all
three. I didn't know what had happened, and I
didn't want to know. I didn't want to be told.
I only felt it was something frightful—something
awful.

"Poor dear! I do believe it'll kill her!" says
Mrs. Hammond, with a click of her tongue meaning pity.

Mr. Baitson turned upon her, more fierce-like
than I'd ever seen him, for he was commonly so
quiet.

"If you can't be silent, Mrs. Hammond, you will
please to leave the room," says he, under his
breath, as it were; and Mrs. Hammond looked all
taken aback, the more as Lady Arthur added—

"Hammond, you forget yourself! How can
you be so unwise?"

And then Lady Arthur did nigh as unwisely
herself, for she stooped down to kiss my forehead,
and burst into tears.

"Hush! No agitation, pray!" Mr. Baitson
says, in the same voice.

But somehow that kiss of Lady Arthur's, being
uncommon and unexpected, woke me up, and my
memory too. In a moment I saw the train rushing up, and father standing on the line, and I tried
to shriek "Father!" but the word wouldn't come.
I think I struggled up, sitting, and somebody got

hold of my hand, and then I seemed to *hear* the buffer strike poor father, and everything turned again into a black mist.

I don't seem to have any clear remembrance of the next coming-to, except that I was in bed, and a sort of horror was on me, and I called for mother, and she didn't come. Then I got so tired, I didn't know how to bear myself, nor how to lie; and Mr. Baitson gave me something to drink; and after that I seemed to go off sound asleep.

I haven't a notion how long the sleep lasted. It might have been hours, or days, or weeks, if I'm to tell from my own feelings.

When I woke up, it was night. I was in my bed still, and a candle was burning. Somebody was leaning back in a chair, sound asleep. I sat up slowly, and looked at her, and I made out gradually that it was Mrs. Hammond.

I didn't want Mrs. Hammond, and I didn't want her to speak to me. I had woke up better, and quite clear in mind. Only I had a feeling that I mustn't let myself think yet about what was come to us.

Something had happened—something dreadful—and down in my heart I knew what it was. But I tried to think I didn't know. I wanted to see and speak to mother. And if I began to think about the *other*, I shouldn't be able.

I got out of bed, stepping softly, and put on my dressing-gown. It wasn't easy, I was that weak and shaken; but still I did it. And I took the candle in my hand, swaying as I walked, for I could scarce keep myself upright. Passing the glass, I had a glimpse of such a white changed face. It didn't look like Kitty Phrynne. But I went straight to the door, and out upon the landing.

There wasn't a sound nor a stir outside, except that the floor creaked beneath me. I waited a moment, and listened.

Father and mother's room was opposite, and the door stood ajar. I had a sort of wonder—were they both sleeping there quietly?

Well, they wouldn't hear me, if I peeped in. I thought I would: just to make sure all was right. Mother would tell me I was silly, but that wouldn't matter.

I said all this to myself, in my thoughts, knowing it wasn't true, yet somehow half believing it.

When I pushed open the door of the room, I found it dark within. So I went softly on towards the bed, carrying my candle, and I found it hadn't been slept in.

I stayed a moment, looking, and feeling, oh so strange! I didn't know what to *let* myself think.

Then I saw I wasn't alone. Somebody was sitting in a chair near the fireplace; sitting still, her hands folded together. I went a step or two nearer, and stopped again. For it was mother; and I was frightened to see mother like that, all alone in the dark, not stirring nor speaking.

She hadn't undressed; and her face was pale, with a sort of stiffened look. But she wasn't unconscious; for her eyes were following me about, staring hard in a cold dull way. I had never seen her so before.

"Mother!" I said, and I went nearer.

But she didn't answer.

I said again "Mother!"

There wasn't a movement, only her eyes were on me still.

Then I came almost close. I wanted to take her hand. I did so crave a kiss, and a word of comfort.

But all of a sudden she drew her chair back.

"Keep off!" says she, in a rough voice, quite hoarse, not like mother's.

I began to shake all over, and turned queer again.

"Mother, don't you know me?" says I. "It's your little Kitty. Don't you know me?"

"Keep off!" says she, just in the same way.

I think if I hadn't been able to cry, I must have fainted again; but I found myself the next moment sobbing most dreadfully, not able to stop, and holding on to the foot of the bed, not able to stand alone.

Mother didn't stir, nor show any pity. She only kept her eyes fixed in that cold stare.

But my sobbing woke up Mrs. Hammond, and she bustled across into mother's room in no time.

"Dear, dear, dear me!" says she, in a fluster,

and half-vexed. "Kitty, whatever are you after?" says she; "coming in here, and you wasn't to leave your bed! Why, Mrs. Phrynne, you don't mean to say you're up and dressed still, and it's two o'clock in the morning. So particular as I begged you to make haste into bed!—now, didn't I? I don't know whatever in the world Mr. Baitson 'll say to me, that I don't," says she.

"Take that girl away," says mother, stern-like.

"Take Kitty away! Why, so I will," says Mrs. Hammond. "Poor little Kitty! she isn't fit to be up, I'm sure—nor you neither, for the matter of that. Come, you'll make haste into bed now, won't you? And Kitty's going to get to sleep again. Give her a kiss now before she goes, won't you, Mrs. Phrynne?"

But mother said "No!" as hard as could be, and turned her head away.

I didn't know how to bear it. I threw myself down on the floor at her feet, and I cried in a sort of shriek, "O mother, mother, forgive me! O mother, love me!" But she wouldn't say one word, and only pushed her chair farther back out of my reach.

Mrs. Hammond pulled me up, and got me somehow across the passage, pretty near carrying me, I think.

"It's no manner of use talking to your mother," says she. "Don't you see she isn't her proper self? The shock's turned her brain, I do believe; and she won't have nothing to do with you yet. I don't know whatever Mr. Baitson 'll say to me if I don't get her into bed, and she's as obstinate as a mule; but I've got to go and try again. She wouldn't let me stay before, and I'm sure I'd no notion I was going to drop to sleep. Dear, dear me, it's a terrible state of things. Now you just lie still, Kitty, and don't you worry about your mother. She'll be better soon, I make no doubt."

I lay still, as I was told, for I was past doing anything else; but as for not worrying—well, I suppose Mrs. Hammond didn't really mean it. She had to say something, and that did as well as anything else.

Worry is hardly the word either. It was so much deeper than "worry."

I had no more sleep that night. Was it likely I should?

The blow that had fallen seemed too dreadful to be borne. My father, my kind gentle good father, gone from us in one moment, without warning, without good-bye! And to think that the last days of his life had been darkened and embittered by my ill-conduct and deceit! If it hadn't been for those last words, and that last kiss of forgiveness, I think I *must* have died of remorse. The pain would have been more than I could bear.

The thought that his death itself might have been in part owing to what I had done—I mean to his mind being over-full—didn't come to torture me till later. I had enough to bear without that— more than enough. As I lay through the slow hours of the early morning, racked with looking back and looking forward, I did feel as if my heart must break—as if I couldn't live through the time that was coming.

When Mr. Baitson called, he said I must keep still, and not think of getting up; and, indeed, I had lost all wish to move. I only wanted to lie still, and to think of father's last kiss. That was my one comfort, though tears came in floods with the recollection. But if I hadn't spoken to him then, oh, how could I ever have borne it?

"Kitty, you must not leave your room again without my leave," says Mr. Baitson.

" No, I won't," I said; " but I want mother! I want mother!"

" I hope she will be able to come to you soon," he says gently. " Not for a day or two, at all events."

" Is mother ill?" I asked.

" Yes," he said. " There are different sorts of illness, Kitty. Such a shock must tell upon her, you know. I would rather have seen her bodily more ill, than this."

I didn't know what he meant, and I was too weak to ask.

" Somebody is coming to take care of you, whom you will be glad to see," he went on.

I didn't ask who. It only seemed so odd he should speak of me being " glad " about anything. I couldn't think I ever should feel " glad " again.

And yet he was in the right. I knew it, two

hours later, when my bedroom door opened, and
Mary Russell walked in.

She looked so pale, and her eyes were red with
crying. But when she sat down on the bed, and
took me into her arms, I did feel a sort of rest that
was almost like gladness.

"My poor Kitty!" she whispered.

"I don't think I believe it," I said, looking up
in her face. "I don't think it's true."

Then I broke down, and cried pitifully. But
soon I said again, "It isn't true. It can't be true.
I think we shall wake up."

"Yes, by-and-by," she said. "When we wake
up in heaven, all sorrow over. That will be a
wonderful awakening, Kitty," says she. "And,
dear, you'll come there to meet *him*," says she.

"O Mary, you won't go! you won't leave us!"
I begged; for I felt as if there was nobody else to
rest on.

"No," she answered. "I am come to stay, so
long as you both want me."

"Mother wants you," I said. "She doesn't love
me any more."

"Kitty, it is not that," Mary answered. "You
mustn't think it for a moment. Your poor mother
isn't fully herself with the trouble. If she could
cry she would be better, but she can't shed a tear,
and till she does——"

"She wouldn't kiss me," I said. "Oh, I know I
deserve it. I know it's the punishment."

Mary let me say so much, and then she told me

not to talk any more. She whispered softly something about the love of God, and how He would take care of us all.

The difference of having her there! But nothing could lighten the great heavy load of pain.

We did not speak of Walter. His name never once came up. I thought of him, yet hardly cared to ask or hear. I could only feel that my father was gone. Everything to do with Walter seemed so small and far away—except the sorrow he and I had caused to father those last few days.

I was in bed about a fortnight, not able to get up: not regularly ill, but too weak and knocked down for anything else. And all that fortnight mother never came into my room.

She was up and about, I knew that. I could hear her step on the stairs, slow and dragging, but still mother's step. She was busy about the house, doing her usual work; and Mr. Baitson said it was better for her than sitting still to brood, though she often did that too.

Yes, I heard her step, but not her voice. Scarce a word passed her lips from morning till night. She was affectionate to Mary in a sort of dull dreary way, but she didn't talk to her nor any one. And she never so much as asked how I was. If Mary spoke of me, mother turned away.

All this wasn't told me at the time. It came later to my hearing.

They couldn't keep mother from the funeral;

not Mr. Baitson, nor anybody. Go she would; and when they tried to hinder, a fierce look came into her eyes. Mr. Baitson said the excitement of being stopped might be worse for her than being let to go; and he gave in.

She didn't shed a tear, all through the Service, nor by the grave. Some hoped she might; but she didn't.

By the time a fortnight was over, I was getting better, and Mr. Baitson used to let me sit up for an hour or two, by way of change. Then Mary got me downstairs; but it was when mother had gone out.

"How soon am I to see mother again?" I said at last to Mary.

"Are you fit for it yet?" said she.

"I don't see why not," I said. I had a sort of hopeless feeling, as if I never should care much about anything again, one way or another. But of course things had to be got through.

"I'm afraid it will give you pain. She isn't like herself yet."

"Will she be—ever?" I asked. "Will she always be vexed with me?"

"It is not exactly being vexed," Mary answered.

"No, it's worse," I said, sighing. "She can't get over the trouble I was to—to *him*." And then I had one of my crying fits; and Mary comforted me. But when it was over I came back to what we had been talking about, and I said, "I do think I ought to see poor mother."

"Yes," Mary answered, slow-like, as if she

wasn't sure. "Yes, that is what I feel; and Mr. Baitson has given leave. If you wish it, and if I think best—but he doesn't want you to be pressed. And he can't promise it will do her good. He does not believe it will do her harm."

"Is mother ill?" I asked.

"Not exactly ill," Mary said. "She isn't ill in body. The blow seems all to have fallen on her poor mind. I don't mean that she's out of her mind, you know. There's nothing to be frightened about; only she's in a kind of stupefied state, and one can't rouse her. She can't see things straight, and there's no getting certain notions out of her head. She is in what the doctors call a 'morbid' state. We hope she will be better by-and-by."

"I don't know what 'morbid' is," I said.

"I think it means that her mind is sick instead of her body," Mary said. "And we have to be very patient with her."

"May I see her?" I asked.

"Yes," Mary says again. "In a day or two, before you go away."

"Am I going?" I asked, still with the dull feeling that I didn't care.

"Yes, you are to have a change. I don't think you'll guess where," says Mary, trying to smile.

"Where?" I asked. "With you, Mary?"

"No, dear; I must see after your mother," Mary said. "No, it's Mrs. Withers you're going to. Mrs. Withers has asked you to her house for a visit. You remember Mrs. Withers, Mr. Arm-

strong's sister-in-law." Ah, didn't I remember the
only time I'd seen her! But Mary went on: "Mr.
Armstrong's wife was her sister, and Mrs. Withers'
husband has a living a few miles out of Littleburgh.
You are to go there for two or three weeks, to be
fed up and taken care of; and you will help a little
with the children."

"I don't want to go. I want to be with you," I
said, mournful enough.

"You will come back to me by-and-by," Mary
says.

"Here! Will you be here still?" I wanted to
know.

Mary didn't speak directly.

"No, not here," she said. "There will have to
be changes."

"What changes?" I asked, getting frightened.

"Dear Kitty, haven't you ever thought," says
she, "that you and your mother can't stay on here?
The house will be wanted for—somebody else."

For another stationmaster in my father's place.
I had not thought of that, and it broke me down
afresh. To leave our home, the dear little home
where *he* had always been; it seemed more than I
could bear.

"Kitty, there's only one way to take it," Mary
whispered. "God sends the trouble, and it is His
will. If you will have it from His Hand, He will
give comfort with the pain."

But in those days I only loved my own will, not
the will of my Heavenly Father.

We didn't say any more then, for I had had
enough. Still, I was not satisfied, and I kept
thinking over all that had to be, and later in the
day I asked Mary—

" Where will mother and I have to live ? "

" Nothing is settled yet," Mary answered. " We
shall see better in a few weeks. When you are
gone to Mrs. Withers, I shall take Mrs. Phrynne to
my old home."

Take mother to Littleburgh! I didn't notice
the word "old," or I should not have been so surprised. To think of mother under the same roof
with Walter Russell did astonish me.

" Not Littleburgh, but Bristol," Mary said
gravely. " Littleburgh would not do. Mr. Baitson
wants her to be in some quite new place, away from
all that reminds her of her trouble. We think
Bristol will be best; and friends are so kind in
giving help."

" And can you be away all this time from——"
I said, and stopped, the colour coming over my face.
I hadn't spoken or heard of her brother since my
father's death.

" Yes," Mary said; and she didn't speak a word
more. I could not understand her look. It meant
something particular, I didn't know what.

Three days later, when I was just dressed,
having got up for the first time before dinner,
Mary said—

" Now I am going to take you downstairs.'

o

"To see mother," I said in a whisper.

"Yes," said she; "unless you would rather not."

"I don't know. I think I ought," I said; but I felt shaky.

"I think so, too," says she. "It may do your mother good. And, Kitty," says she, "you've got to put yourself out of sight, and try to be brave. Don't mind if she turns from you at first. Just walk into the kitchen quite naturally, and speak to her exactly as usual."

I promised to try; but as we went downstairs I clung tight to her, frightened to think what was coming. I'm not sure that Mary didn't feel a sort of fear too, she looked so pale.

"Now, Kitty," she whispers, outside the kitchen, "don't you mind anything, but go straight up to her, and be like your own self."

Easier said than done; but I did my best. I opened the door, and went to the table, where mother was ironing, though I felt as if my legs wouldn't carry me there.

"Mother!" I said.

She looked up at me, and down again. Her face had the sort of fixed look I'd seen the first night; and her black dress and widow's cap made her so strange.

"Speak!" I heard Mary whisper.

"Mother!" I said, "I haven't seen you for ever so long. Mayn't I have a kiss?"

But she went on ironing, hard and fast.

Mary came close, and put an arm round my waist.

"Mrs. Phrynne," says she cheerfully, and I did wonder at her for being so cheerful — "Mrs. Phrynne, Kitty has been ill, and she is going away to-morrow. Mayn't she have a kiss before she goes?"

Mother didn't answer one word.

"Come, Kitty, give your mother a kiss," says Mary, leading me.

I did as I was bid, and mother bore the kiss, but that was all, scarce stopping a moment in her work, and showing not a sign of pleasure. I couldn't bear it, hardly, and I was ready to drop. Mary gave me a chair, and I set off sobbing, and presently I saw mother had left her ironing and was standing to watch me in a queer sort of way as if she couldn't make me out.

"Poor Kitty," Mary says.

Mother came near, looking hard still.

"Kitty! Yes, it's Kitty," says she.

"Your own Kitty," Mary says.

"Yes, it's Kitty," mother says, but not as if she cared.

"O mother, *do* love me," I broke out, feeling so miserable.

"I've got no heart to love anybody," mother says, and she turned off back to her ironing. "*He's* gone," said she.

"And he loved and forgave Kitty," Mary says, slow and quiet.

"Maybe," mother answered; and she took up her iron, but didn't use it.

"He forgave Kitty," Mary says again.

"Maybe," mother answered short; "but she broke his heart first."

And not one word more would mother say to Mary nor me after that. Mary gave up trying to make her, for the doctor had said she mustn't press matters too far. I went to my room, and felt as if everything was gone, and nothing was left to live for.

In the morning I mustered up courage to ask Mr. Baitson about mother, and whether she would ever be her proper self again. He said he hoped she would; but it must take time. The dreadful shock of seeing father killed had had a strange effect upon her mind, so she seemed to see everything crooked, and couldn't be argued with. Only time and change could cure her. He told me I must do my best to get well and strong quickly, so as to be able to take care of poor mother.

I was not allowed to see mother again; Mr. Baitson said it was better not to excite her. Mr. Armstrong looked in for a few kind words with me as he had done often; but I never could bear yet to see him, without crying too much for speech. It made me think so of that last talk before poor father was killed.

Early after dinner Mary started with me, as I was hardly fit to travel all the way alone. Mary had things to do in Littleburgh, she said, and wouldn't be back till late; so Mrs. Bowman was left in charge of mother.

We got out at Littleburgh Station together, and there Mary put me into a fly to drive to Deane Rectory. I remember how she kissed me, and told me to be brave.

Then I drove off alone, feeling dreary; and the fly wasn't two minutes away from the station before I passed somebody I knew.

It was Walter Russell!

One wouldn't have believed, after all that had passed, that I should have cared for him still. But I did. Seeing him walk along the pavement, with his sort of jaunty air, sent a shock all through me, and I could have cried out his name. I did lean forward, and he looked up, and his eyes met mine.

But there was no sign of knowing me, not the very least. He didn't smile nor nod.

The next moment, and while I was driving by, he stopped short to speak to a young girl, seeming as pleased as could be. The way he fixed his eyes on her, admiring, was the very same way exactly that he was used to do it to me.

I don't know whether I was most hurt or most angry. I couldn't get over the great wrong he had done, making me deceive my father and mother; yet I liked him still. I couldn't feel real respect, and I knew well I ought not to think about him any more; yet the very name of Walter Russell had a strange power over me.

If he had given me his old look and smile, I'm not sure but he might have bent me again to his will, and in time led me further into evil.

He didn't, happily! And oh, it's good for us that things don't always happen as we'd choose.

But if any more was needed to make me feel quite hopeless and wretched, it was that sight of Walter, just after leaving Mary, when mother seemed to have no love left for her Kitty, and everything was changed.

Doesn't God sometimes strip us for a while of all joy and pleasure, just to make us turn to Him? I do think He does, when it's needful, out of His great Fatherly love. And I think it was needful for me. Nothing less would have brought me to His Feet. So long as I had any earthly prop to cling to, I would have clung there.

In that lonesome five miles' drive, it seemed as if every prop was gone.

I don't think I cried. I had shed such lots of tears lately, I must have pretty near cried them all away. I only sat still, gazing at the hedges, and wondering if I should ever have any brightness in life again.

Well, some amount of brightness didn't lie far ahead, but then one can't see ahead. There's never any knowing what'll come next.

It was raining when I reached the Rectory, and I got out and stood in the passage as forlorn as could be.

The maid saw my box brought in, and then——

" 'I am not making fun of *you*,' she said, as if afraid I should be offended
at her."—*Page* 215.

"I'll tell my mistress you've come," says she, and she went off somewhere.

I wondered how long I should have to wait, and while I was waiting, a little girl came out through a door.

She was nine years old then, and I never can forget that first sight of her. She had been dressing up for a game with her brothers, and a green silk scarf was twisted round her fair hair. It was such a merry rosy little face, all full of fun and laughter.

When she saw me she didn't turn grave. She came and stood in front of me, laughing still.

"I'm not making fun of *you*," she said, as if she was afraid I should be hurt. "Only we *have* had such a game, and they took me for a baboon. Wasn't that comical? As if a baboon could wear a scarf!"

Then a puzzled look came into her eyes.

"Oh, I thought you were somebody else," she said. "I thought it was nurse's niece. Do you want to see my father or mother?"

"I'm only Kitty Phrynne," I said, for I didn't know what else to reply.

"Kitty Phrynne!" says she. And such a look of pity and tenderness came as was wonderful in a child's face. She stopped laughing, and her eyes were grave in a moment. "Kitty Phrynne! Oh, —I know!"

The sort of sigh between those words! I don't know how it was, but I felt as if she understood.

"Does mother know you've come?" she asked.
"I think she's been told," I said.
"Yes,"—and she stopped. "Mother is busy,"
—and she stopped again. "Mother will like me
to take care of you. Poor Kitty Phrynne!" says
she, such a soft look in her eyes. "*Poor* Kitty
Phrynne! I'm Kathleen Withers."

She took hold of my hand, and made me come
towards the staircase.

"Miss Kathleen!" says the maid, turning up
again. "I was trying to find you. Mistress is
busy for a few minutes, and she says will you
please look after the young person till she can
come."

"Yes; of course. It's all right," says the child.
"I'm going to take Kitty Phrynne to her bedroom.
And I want her to have some tea, please, as quick
as possible." Then I heard another sigh. "*Poor*
Kitty Phrynne!" whispered the child.

Wasn't it strange how that comforted me, and
took away the lonesome feeling?

CHAPTER XI.

IN CHURCH.

THAT little Miss Kathleen Withers was the very sweetest child!

She seemed to come to me like a sort of sunbeam. I had got out of sunshine, and among shadows, with black clouds overhead, and I couldn't see any brightness anywhere. And then all of a sudden I came on her.

Isn't it wonderful how comfort is sent when one needs it? Not that I deserved anything of the sort, I'm sure; but still it seemed sent.

Mrs. Withers was kept longer than she meant or thought to be. But it didn't matter. I was in no hurry.

Miss Kathleen took me up to a little attic-room, as neat as could be, and told me I was to sleep there. She popped her head into different rooms by the way, bidding me peep in, and telling me whose they were. "That's father and mother's," she'd say. "And that's the best spare-room. And that's mine. And that's the boys'. And those are the nurseries."

When I was in my room, she ran away; but

before I'd been five minutes alone, she came rapping at the door, and when I opened it, she was carrying a little tray, with a cup of tea and some bread and butter.

"That's for you," says she, all in a glow of pleasure.

"O Miss Kathleen, you shouldn't!" I said, feeling shamed to have her wait on me.

"O yes, I should," said she, walking in. "They'd have brought it, but I wanted to bring it myself. Why shouldn't I?" says she, looking up at me. "You're in trouble, you know; and father always says one ought to wait upon people in trouble, and take care of them. And you've been ill too. Oh, don't cry," says she, looking anxious. "I oughtn't to have said that, ought I? Please don't cry, but just drink the tea while it is hot. You see, the servants don't have their tea for nearly an hour yet, and we thought you oughtn't to wait so long."

Then she bade me sit down on the bed, and she perched herself on the dressing-table.

"Don't you like tables to sit on? I do," said she. "I like anything better than chairs."

I wasn't used to sit on tables, and I said so, my tears drying fast, for she interested me.

"Well, I suppose I shall have to leave off soon, now I'm growing so big," says she. "I wish one needn't grow big. Only of course, when I'm big I can be of more use to my mother and father, and that will be nice."

Then she told me she was the only girl, and she gave me the names and ages of her brothers, and all the birthdays. She seemed to think a deal of the birthdays. She talked next about the pets— the dogs and cats and birds—and she said she wasn't fond of lessons, only she tried to work hard because one ought.

"For I want to be very very useful by-and-by to everybody," said she, "and of course I can't be that if I don't learn now. Don't *you* want to be useful?" says she, smiling up at me as if she'd known me always.

"I suppose I do," I said, wondering that I hadn't wanted it more.

"Only 'suppose,'" says she, opening her eyes wide. "Oh, but I want it a great deal more than only just supposing. I want it dreadfully. Don't you know those words"—and then she folded her hands, speaking soft—"don't you know those words about our Lord?—'He went about doing good.' That's what I want," says she. "I want to go about doing good, when I'm grown up. Mother says, if I mean to do it by-and-by, I've got to begin now, because there's so much in habit. Do you think I shall be able to do any good to *you* while you're here?" says she, not a bit conceited, but all in earnest.

"Yes, Miss Kathleen," said I, for I did feel as if she was doing me good already.

"But then I'm only a little girl," says she. "Mother will do you good, and father. I don't see

how I can. I'm only a little girl, and you are
grown up. Anyhow "—and she smiled—"anyhow, I can bring you a cup of tea, and a cup of tea
does you good, I'm sure. It's put more colour
into your face already, you know."

It wasn't only the cup of tea, though. It was
her own self. She had brought a sort of gleam of
hope to me for the first time—even though that
very day Walter Russell had turned from me.

Mrs. Withers was just as kind as Miss Kathleen,
though in a different manner. I liked her, but I
never could forget the one time we had met before.
Most like she didn't forget it neither. People
don't forget that sort of thing, once it's come before
them, and of course she must know I'd been deceiving them that day. She must have heard all
about it since, which made her asking me to the
house the more kind. I used to wonder sometimes
if everything had been told, and I couldn't feel
sure.

Miss Kathleen took a wonderful fancy to me.
She used to find me out wherever I was, and bring
me a flower from her garden, or a book from her
bookcase, or else she'd come and sit down for a
chat, which I liked best of all. She seemed to
have got it into her head that I was in trouble and
that she had to comfort me, and she was always
trying one way and another. "Mother is so busy,"
she'd say. "I do like to help her." But I think
she got fond of me too.

There wasn't any difficulties made by Mrs.

Withers. She just let things go on so. But one day, all of a sudden, she took me by surprise, speaking when she and I were alone together. I couldn't think whatever was coming, but soon I understood.

She began about the liking Miss Kathleen showed to be with me, and how she was very glad Miss Kathleen should—only—and there she stopped, and began afresh. Miss Kathleen was such a good truthful child always, she said, and so simple, and with no nonsense in her head. Then there came another stop.

"Kitty," says she, "you have not always been truthful, and you have had a great deal of nonsense in your head. I know so much, you see. Can I depend upon you with my little girl?" says she. "You have had a sharp lesson, and I think you cannot be the same after it that you were before. If I let the child be in and out with you as much as she likes, can I be sure that she will gain no harm—will learn no deceit nor folly from you?" says she.

It did go to my heart to think I wasn't counted fit to be trusted with that child; and yet what else was to be expected, after the way I'd let myself be drawn into evil?

I don't half know what I said, except that I *had* had a sharp lesson, and I would be very very careful, and never speak a word to Miss Kathleen which I wouldn't wish her mother to hear.

"Yes, that will be right—that will do," said she.

Then I gave way and cried bitterly, and how good, to be sure, she was! She took one seat, and made me take another, and she said such comforting words.

Somehow I hadn't felt till then so fully how I had sinned against God first and most of all, and how first and most of all I needed His forgiveness.

I had wronged my father, and before he died he had forgiven me; and I had wronged my mother, and she wasn't in a state to know how to pardon. But far, far beyond these I had wronged my Father in Heaven, and that had been only a second sort of thought with me.

"Against Thee, Thee only, have I sinned!" Mrs. Withers said once or twice; and I began to say the words in my heart, meaning them. Not "only" in one sense, because I had wronged others; but "only" in another sense, because the wrong against others was nothing at all seen beside the wrong done to my God.

I kept thinking of that wrong and sin all the rest of the day. I tried to pray for pardon, but no comfort came. When Miss Kathleen came to me, and wanted to talk about all sorts of things, I didn't find it easy to listen nor answer. "Against Thee— Thee only"—was running through my head.

Next day was Sunday; and it was a day I shan't soon forget, though it passed by quiet enough to all outward seeming, and nobody could have guessed it was anything out of the common to me.

The morning service wasn't. I went to Church,

and knelt and stood and sat just as usual; and I couldn't listen much, nor take it all in. And the afternoon dragged by in a like fashion.

Then came the evening service. I had a seat in a dark corner, half behind a pillar, where I couldn't be seen. I was glad of this—soon.

For in the very first words, the opening sentences, there came a message straight to my heart—

" I will arise, and go to my Father, and will say unto Him, Father, I have sinned——"

That was all I heard.

In one moment I seemed to see the whole. The Father waiting at home, full of love, full of longing; and the poor wanderer far away, just making up his mind to " arise and go."

Perhaps I hadn't done that. I had sat still and bemoaned myself, expecting to have something done to me; but I hadn't taken the first step. I had not said, " I will arise and go."

It might not be many steps to take; still I had to take those steps. They were possible steps for me, because they were right.

" And I will say unto Him, Father——"

There, behind the pillar, in the dimly-lighted country Church, my whole self seemed to give a leap forward, hurrying towards the Father whom I had wronged; and a voice in my heart cried out, "Father!"

It was the cry which had brought to me before the lesser forgiveness which I had craved.

" Father!" I cried, and no man in the congregation heard; but He was listening.

"Father, I have sinned against Thee!" I tried to pray this, and I tried to ask pardon "for Jesus' sake." Then I remembered that Jesus is One with the Father, and that He, as God, is my Father. Isn't He called so once in the Bible, "the Everlasting Father"? Speaking to Him is speaking to God. And no common words of prayer would come, but only the one cry, a child's cry, out of danger and distress—"Father! Father! Father!"

Then the other time came back to me, when I had said the same word, and my earthly father had taken me in his arms, putting away the past, forgiving and showing love.

I thought how it was to be the same over again.

For "when he saw his son a great way off, he ran, and fell on his neck, and kissed him."

So poor and weak, so unworthy of any such love! Could *I* hope or expect——?

I don't know about the hoping or expecting. But I know that was the manner of forgiveness which came to me. I could not stand or sit. I could only kneel, with face hidden, feeling that I *had* arisen, and that my Father's "Everlasting Arms" were around me.

I didn't hear much of the service for a while; when I did, a new light and beauty had come into the prayers.

I think life was changed to me from that day. Having "bread enough and to spare," I wasn't like to care so much for "the husks that the swine do eat."

And yet of course the old temptations wouldn't lose their power at once, and fighting enough might lie ahead. I had arisen and gone back to my Father. That didn't mean that I could not wander off again, if so I was minded, or if I grew careless.

"Kitty, I think you're different from when you first came," Miss Kathleen said soberly one day, near a week later. "You do look more happy, you know. Are you different? and are you happier? and has it done you good being here?"

"Yes, Miss Kathleen," I answered. I could say "Yes" to all three questions. But I couldn't talk about what I felt yet, even to her. It was too sacred and too solemn; and I wasn't worthy. I had to strive to live as a child of God; that was the great matter. Doing and living are far more than mere talking.

P

CHAPTER XII.

ON A PLATFORM.

I HAD been asked to Mrs. Withers' for two or three weeks, but she kept me there for six weeks and more.

Once in every few days I had a letter from Mary. She spoke of mother as better for the change to Bristol, but still as not herself. I wondered if she ever would be her true self again; but Mrs. Withers bade me trust and hope; and I did try, though it wasn't easy.

Mary didn't say much about plans in her letters. I could not make out whether I was to join her and mother in Bristol, or whether we were to meet in Claxton again. Once I asked, and there came no answer to the question. So I let it alone, and just waited, not knowing.

Mrs. Withers had heard from Mr. Armstrong, I knew; and he was sure to have been told everything about mother.

It wasn't so hard to wait, with the new help and life that had come to me.

And yet nobody need suppose that I hadn't plenty of battling, or that doing right was all at once quite easy to me. No such thing. I had to fight hard, and pray hard. But there was the difference that I did pray, and that I was learning how to fight.

Old temptations had power over me yet; of course they had. Was it to be expected they'd die out in a moment?

I was getting to a more true and right notion of what Walter Russell was. He had led me into evil. He had deceived and taught deceit. I saw all this, and I did resolve that, God helping me, there should be nothing further between us, even if he wished it, at least until he should be another sort of man—and nothing at any time hidden from my mother.

But still I couldn't at once cast aside all thoughts of him. I do believe there's an unhealthy power which some people have over some others, and which makes the breaking loose from them a hard matter. But I believe that anybody who wills *may* break loose from such a bondage, through prayer and resolute doing.

Well, at last I heard I was to go to Bristol. Mary wrote that the doctors were afraid of Claxton for mother yet, and of course Mrs. Withers couldn't be expected to keep me on for any length of time. Besides, it was right I should go to mother, now I was all right in health, and strong again. Mary didn't say this; but I felt it.

The puzzle to me was how Mary had managed to be so long away from her brother. She never so much as said his name in her letters, and I knew she had taken to dressmaking again among her old friends.

The six weeks at Deane Rectory had been a wonderful help to me; and so had Mr. Withers' teaching, though I haven't said anything about that. His sermons were beautiful, and now and then he'd say a thing in passing that stayed by one for days.

But the one I minded most of all leaving was little Miss Kathleen. She cried, and so did I, when we said good-bye; and she promised to write long letters to me, and made me promise I'd write to her.

The through-train for Bristol left Littleburgh at twelve o'clock, and I got there a good while before, being driven in the little light cart which was often in and out for all sorts of purposes. The man had a lot of things to do, so we started early; and I had to wait a good time at the station —something near three-quarters of an hour, I believe.

I had a little book to read which Miss Kathleen had given me; and I sat down on a quiet bench, in a corner, with it open on my knee.

All of a sudden a queer sort of feeling came over me; for there on the platform, not far off, was Walter Russell.

He had his jaunty air, and kept moving about with a look of being very important. I don't know why, but he didn't seem to me so much of a gentleman as he'd seemed once. He put on such airs; and when he stopped to speak to somebody, he laughed so loud.

And yet my heart went pit-a-pat, and I was all in a flutter. I hoped he wouldn't see me; but still I didn't know how to bear being passed over by him.

If he did know I was there, he mightn't choose to speak. And that would be the best thing for me. I knew it, yet a longing came into my mind for just a word—only a word! I never could feel sure he had really known me that day I drove by him in the fly.

He went to the other end of the platform, and walked back, keeping up his jaunty air. All of a sudden, he stopped opposite, and our eyes met.

There was nobody near, except one old market-woman, half asleep, at the other end of the bench.

"Hallo! Why, it's Kitty Phrynne!" says he; and his mouth dropped open in a sort of amaze. He didn't look delighted. I could see that plain enough.

I did not move, or get up. All at once, clear like a bell, I seemed to hear mother's voice saying her favourite saying—"Least said, soonest mended!"

"Least said, soonest mended!" And I sat still, determined I'd not be drawn into any folly. I *would* show mother I had some self-respect. I had nothing more to do with Walter, nor he with me; and the less we said to each other the better. If I got into a talk, I couldn't depend on myself.

"I declare it's—Kitty," says he again. And I kept still. I wouldn't stir.

"Come! come! you don't bear malice, I hope," says he, and he came up to shake hands.

"Bear malice! What for?" said I slowly. I thought I'd keep strict to the "least said" plan.

"What for! Oh, come! that's good," he broke out, with a laugh.

He meant about the watch, of course—but I did wonder he could laugh.

"I don't see anything to make fun of," I said.

"Well, no—nor do I," says he. "Most serious event in a man's life, isn't it?"

And he sat down by my side. "Kitty, you're prettier than ever," says he softly.

But that was going too far. I couldn't stand it. Something in his manner and speech angered me; and I thought how *he* had led me into saddening my father's last days—how perhaps even, but for him, father might have been living still, and mother well, and I a happy girl in the dear old home! No; that was going too far!

"Good-bye," I said. "My train will start soon." And I got up and walked away.

But he was at my side.

"Kitty—Kitty—I didn't mean to vex you," says he, in a sort of wheedling manner. "Just say you're not vexed. Say we can be friends still."

"Friends!" I said, and I turned to look at him. I hadn't a wish for any more soft words. A change seemed to have come over me. Perhaps it

had been coming long, though I didn't find it out
till then. "Friends!" I said.

"Well, yes," said he. "We've been friends,
haven't we?"

And I said—I couldn't help it, for the words
seemed to be squeezed out of me, I thinking of my
poor father—

"No! You've been the worst enemy I ever
had."

I didn't add another word. "*Least said*—" was
sounding in a whisper somewhere. I had to say
enough, but not too much. There's never any
good in piling on a lot of words, if one dozen are
all that's wanted.

"Kitty!" says he, as if he was confounded.

I didn't speak.

"You don't mean that," says he, wheedling
again.

But I held my tongue.

"Kitty, I do assure you I couldn't help it," says
he. "I didn't mean to take you in."

"When you said it was lent—and then to have
sold it!" says I slowly.

"Lent! Sold it!" says he, looking uncomfortable, and then he gave a sort of laugh. "Oh, I
see—you mean that wretched watch," says he.

And I just said "Yes."

"But I thought you meant something else," says
he. "Mary has told you——"

"Mary has told me nothing at all," I said.

And I turned and walked away once more. He

didn't follow me this time. I saw he was all taken aback like, to find I thought so much of his dishonesty.

The train was waiting, and I got into a third-class carriage. I felt so glad that talk was over, and so glad I hadn't said more. Mother would be pleased, I thought—some day when I could tell her. It wouldn't do to speak Walter Russell's name in her hearing yet awhile.

I had to sit a good while in the carriage, waiting; but Walter didn't come near me again. Presently I caught sight of him sauntering along the platform; and then a smart sort of girl joined him. He put his arm through hers, and she laughed and joked in a shrill voice. I didn't like her look.

After that they went out of sight. I believed it was the same girl I had seen him speak to, the day I drove from Littleburgh to Deane Rectory; but I could not be sure. I hadn't noticed her then so much as him.

The train started, and there was nobody in the compartment with me. I had it to myself. Presently I found myself saying aloud—

"That is all over!"

The words did not mean pain. I had a feeling of being set free from bondage. So often I had felt that I couldn't break loose from Walter's mastery; yet here was I loose, and the mastery gone. I had so feared to meet him; yet now we had met, and he had not his old power over me.

I did not know whether he was changed or I was changed; but either way I knew it was an answer to prayer. For I *had* prayed.

All through the journey to Bristol I was feeling so glad and thankful, so happy to be free.

It was a long journey. The train stopped at pretty nearly every station, and people got in and out. All of them were civil to me; and one old woman took me under her care, begging me to eat a lot of rich plum-cake. But I had been well supplied with sandwiches and cake before I left Deane Rectory.

Bristol station was reached at last; and an uncommon big bustling place it seemed to be, different as could be from Claxton. I felt very lone and strange, till I caught sight of Mary's face on the platform; and then it was all right.

"Are you ready for a good walk, Kitty?" she asked.

I said "Yes," for I was cramped with long sitting. So we settled about having my box sent, and Mary and I started off. We could have done a good part of the way by tram, if we'd been minded; but I liked the walk, and there was no harm in saving a few pence.

The rooms Mary had taken for my mother and herself were not actually near the part that had been her girlhood's home; not down in Bristol, but higher up in Redland. Mary had feared the narrow streets and noise of Bristol for my mother. Still she had found out all her old friends, and had

had lots of kindness from them, as well as getting plenty of work.

She told me this as we toiled up one of the steep hills out of Bristol, with houses on both sides, and houses around everywhere.

"I shouldn't like to live down there," I said.

"No; it isn't as if you'd been used to the place always," Mary answered.

Then I asked, "Will mother be pleased to see me?"

"I can't tell yet, but I hope so, Kitty. She seemed glad this morning, when I told her you were coming."

"She hasn't ever written to me," I said.

"No; she has written to nobody. She doesn't seem able. But she keeps the rooms nice, so as to leave me free for work; and sometimes she works too."

"I'm sure I can never thank you enough for staying with her all this time," I said. "I couldn't have thought you'd have been able."

"Things are changed," Mary said.

I didn't know what she meant. I looked for more, but she wouldn't speak. So I said—

"How soon will mother and I have to go back to Claxton?"

"Do you wish very much to go?" she asked.

"I don't know. Yes," I said. "Claxton is our home." And yet I felt it would be sad, with everything so different.

"Could Claxton be home to you again, I

wonder?" says she. "In another house, and without your father?"

"Mother wouldn't like to live anywhere else," I said.

"Yes; she will be content with whatever is decided."

"But when you go home to Littleburgh?"

"I am not going to Littleburgh. I have no home there now," she answered.

I was that startled with her words, I came to a standstill on the pavement.

"Not got any home in Littleburgh?"

"No," said she. "That's one of the things that are changed."

But what was to become of Walter, all alone there?

"Kitty, I haven't spoken of my brother to you lately," said she, as I was thinking this.

"No," I said, "not once."

"I thought it might be best not," she said. "Perhaps the time is come now to speak."

"I saw him at Littleburgh station to-day," I said.

"You did?" said she.

And I looked up, and our eyes met. Mary must have seen something in my face which pleased her, for she broke into a smile.

"He was on the platform," I said; "and we had a few words. I didn't say much; I thought mother would rather I shouldn't. He talked about hoping I didn't bear malice. I fancied he meant the watch, you know, but he didn't; and I don't know what he did mean. And he asked if we could be friends still; and I said he had been my enemy. He seemed sure I had heard something about him from you, and I said I had not. And then I walked away."

"Right!" Mary said.

"But what did he mean?"

"He meant—that he has treated you as he has treated a good many girls," she said. "He is married."

"Married!"

I didn't feel as if it was a blow, or hard to bear. I almost felt like laughing, when I remembered the things I had said, and how he had looked.

"Yes. Are you sorry for your own sake, Kitty?" asked she. "I think you have had an escape to be thankful for."

"I do think so too," I answered; and I spoke from my heart.

"Ah, that is right, that is right," said she. "Then you understand now. But I have not told you all. Walter married three weeks after I left him, to take care of you and your mother. My dear, it would have been just the same if I had stayed there," says she. "He was bent on having the girl, and I knew it. He married her, saying nothing to me. And a week later——"

"Is she a nice girl?" I asked.

"No; not a nice girl at all," Mary said; and her face took its stern look for just a moment.

" Not a girl I could wish to live with, even if she wished to have me ; which she does not."

" And they are living at Littleburgh," I said in a sort of dreamy way. It all seemed so queer.

" At Littleburgh, but not in our old home. Walter was dismissed from his situation within a week of being married. Yes, dismissed. He had been falsifying the school accounts. Of course he quite forfeited all hope of another situation as schoolmaster."

" And he has nothing to live on ? "

" He has something just now. His wife has a few hundreds of her own. She is an orphan. I suppose they will spend all they have, and then———" Mary sighed. " My poor Walter ! " she said. " Yes, I love him still—unhappy boy ! But I do not respect him. How can I ? "

I don't think I made any answer. I was thinking what an escape I had had of being his wife ! That had grown plain to me at last.

" So I have come back to my old haunts," she said, " and to old friends. The question is now— shall I live alone, or will you and your mother live with me ? "

" O Mary !—may we ? " I cried. " May we— always ? "

" I should like it," she answered. " I love your mother dearly—and you too," though I could see that was the afterthought. " Why shouldn't you take to dressmaking ? " says she. " But I am afraid there wouldn't be work enough in Claxton."

CHAPTER XIII.

WITH MY MOTHER.

THE house where Mary stopped was of red brick, old-fashioned and stiff-looking, and it stood on an old-fashioned terrace, raised high above the road. There was one window beside the door, and two windows above, and two windows again over that.

"Is the whole of the house yours?" I asked, thinking it wasn't a pretty house, after my dear old country home.

"No," said she. "Only the dining-room and two back bedrooms."

Then she went in, leading the way. It was a narrow dark sort of passage, with faded oilcloth on the floor. I groped along after her; and when she turned into the first room, that was almost as dark, Mary struck a light, and nobody was there except ourselves.

"Your mother must be upstairs," said she. "Sit down, Kitty."

I did as she bade me, tired enough to be glad to rest after my journey and long walk. I was longing and yet dreading to see mother. What if she turned from me still? if she was always to turn from me for the rest of my life?

Mary put the candle on the mantel-shelf, and it lighted up the room dimly—only a small room, with poor furniture: old black horse-hair chairs, and a black horse-hair sofa, and a table, and a sort of little sideboard.

" I get through my dressmaking in this room," said she. " Happily I have plenty of work—more than I can do alone. I had to refuse two orders only last week. Why shouldn't you and I make a good thing of it, Kitty? " and she smiled, to cheer me up.

" I like pretty work, and mother always says I'm quick. But I shouldn't like to sit all day long in this room."

" Ah, we can't always do just what we like in life," says she quietly; " can we, Kitty? "

" No! " I said.

" The question isn't so much what we like, as what God likes for us," says she.

I got up, and gave her a kiss. " Yes, I'm trying to learn that, Mary, I am really."

" Then you'll be taught it, dear," said she. " God always gives us the teaching we need—if we are willing." And she added in a cheery sort of voice,—" But I don't mean you to work all day long, and never to have a breath of air. There's the Durdham Downs quite close—a great stretch of grass and open sky, ever so much wider than your common—and the river and the rocks and the trees."

"It isn't all houses, only houses, then?" I said.

"No, indeed," Mary answered. "You just wait till you've been over our Downs. Your mother says she never saw anything to equal them in all her life."

"I'm glad! I shan't mind work," I said, trying to be brave. "Shall I come with you to find mother? And am I to sleep with her?"

"Not at first, I think. I shall put you in my little room, and sleep with your mother myself for a few days. No, sit here, Kitty, and rest. I'll bring her to you."

Then Mary was gone; and I stayed alone in the strange room, with everything strange about me; for though we had furniture of our own, it had all been left at Claxton, till we could settle where to go and what to do. I was glad to think we should have our own furniture again some day, and not live among these dingy chairs and tables.

Mary didn't come back. I went to the window and looked out. It was very nearly dark outside by now. The terrace pavement was muddy, for there had been rain, and three boys were playing on it, shouting and pulling one another about.

As I stood there, watching them, a sudden recollection of Rupert came. I couldn't say what brought it, except those boys playing together. Rupert and I had often played together many years before. Or it may have been that I was free at last from bondage to Walter Russell, and so I

could spring back to my old liking and thoughts of
him. Like a piece of whalebone, you know, that's
bent and tied down; but so soon as ever it's untied,
it'll leap out straight as it was before.

His face rose up before me—such a good plain
honest face; and I seemed to see it as I had that
last time with a glow of feeling, only all the anger
and hardness were gone. He had loved me so
truly—so different from Walter Russell, who only
loved himself and made use of me for his own
purposes. Two men couldn't be more unlike and
opposite than those two.

"Poor Rupert!" I sighed; "I wonder what's
become of him! I wonder what he would think
of all these changes!"

And oh, how grieved he would be about father!
I could hardly keep back my tears, picturing this.

"And it was I who drove him away!" I went
on. "I—for the sake of Walter Russell."

I *did* want to see Rupert again—poor Rupert,
whom I had so scorned after all his goodness and
devotion to me. But perhaps I never should: and
even if some day I did, he would not be the same.
He would have forgotten his old liking for Kitty.

"I shall have grown ugly by that time," I
murmured; "and he will have learnt to like somebody else. And it will be just what I deserve."

Then Mary came in.

"Is mother upstairs?" I asked.

Mary looked a little pale and troubled, I
thought.

Q

"No, dear," she said. "Your mother has been out all the afternoon. You and I will have some tea to refresh ourselves, and then I must go and find her."

"But you don't know where she is."

"Not exactly, but I know her favourite haunts. When she walks alone, she almost always goes to one particular part of Durdham Down. I have had to fetch her home before now. She forgets how time goes."

"Then mother isn't well yet?"

"I think there is a touch of weakness still, Kitty. I am not sure that she will ever *quite* lose it," Mary answered.

She made tea quickly, not letting me help : and presently I asked, "May I go with you to look for her?"

"Too far, after your journey," says she.

"O no! I am getting quite rested," I said. "Please don't leave me alone here. Mother might come in."

"Would you be afraid of her, if she did?" asked Mary, with a curious sort of look.

"No," I said, and I was ashamed. "No, not afraid exactly ; only I don't know how she'll take seeing me."

"I think she will be glad," Mary said.

But when I begged still to go, Mary did not say no. She told me I might if I was up to it ; and after a good tea I felt strong. Mary seemed pretty sure mother wouldn't come back while we were away. The same thing had happened before when mother was excited about something; and no doubt the thought of my returning had excited her.

So as soon as we had finished our tea, we started, I keeping close to Mary's side, with a sort of protected feeling which I have always had with her. I think I had it even when she was ill and I was well. For there's no doubt Mary's was the stronger and firmer nature of the two. If I had been brought up by another sort of mother than mine, one who allowed self-indulgence, I should have been turned out a very useless creature.

Mary didn't take me round by Durdham Down, as it was late, but through Redland and Clifton streets, till we got to a part of Clifton Down where it was too dark to see much; only there was grass and trees.

" Tired, Kitty ? " says she.

" No," I answered. " Shall we find mother soon ? "

" Yes, I hope so," said she. " We're almost close to where Clifton Down joins Durdham Down."

" And Durdham Down is where mother goes most," I said.

" Yes; and always to the loneliest parts," said she. " Your mother is a lover of the country, you know."

We had been going along a level road or path a little way, where an avenue of trees grew; but soon we left the trees, turning into a white road, which rose up, with grass downs and scattered bushes on both sides. Mary said that was Durdham Down. Then she stepped up on the grass to the left, and led away over it, among the bushes, on broken ground. I could not see where I went, and I stumbled and clung to her arm, but she seemed to know every step.

"Not much farther, I hope," said she. "Are you frightened?"

"O no," I said; "only it is so dark and so lonely. I shouldn't like to be here by myself. But with you——"

"That makes a difference, doesn't it?" said she. "But I should not have minded coming alone, if it had been my duty. I've done so before!"

"And you would not have been afraid?"

"Perhaps a little nervous," said she. "But if one is doing one's duty, I do think one may always look to be taken care of."

Presently we came out together from among bushes and rocks to a place I didn't expect. There was an iron railing, and beyond the railing a depth going sheer down ever so far. A river lay below, shining in the moonlight, which at that very moment had broken out strong and clear. Beyond the river were high dark banks, covered with woods. It was a strange wild scene altogether to me, seen in the dim light.

Mary went straight to the railing, stepping quick over the roughnesses in our path, though indeed we were in no regular path, but among rocks and bushes and grass ; and she stood there looking about.

"It is a beautiful place," said she.

"I should like it in the day-time," I said.

"I like it always," said she.

"Is this where mother comes to be alone ?" I asked.

"Somewhere about here," said she. "Not far off, commonly."

And she called in a soft voice, which must have carried a good way, the air was so still—

"Mrs. Phrynne ! Mrs. Phrynne !"

But there wasn't any answer.

"Come ! we'll look," Mary answered.

We kept as near to the railings as could be, but sometimes we had to go round a pile of rocks and bushes. Mary and I searched some distance both ways, and all to no good. There wasn't a sign of a living creature.

Once the moon went in, and how dark it was ! I felt chilly and frightened.

"Perhaps she is gone home, and she'll be tired waiting for us," I said.

"I don't think it," Mary answered.

We stood still again, listening, and all at once it came into my head to call, "Mother !"

"Yes—try that, Kitty !" says Mary.

"Mother !" I cried. "Mother ! Mother !"

There was a step among the bushes near us.

"Mother," I cried ; "oh, do come !"

No mistake about the step now. In one
moment more mother herself came out from the
bushes, walking straight towards us. The moon
shone full on her face, and her eyes were wide
open with an eager look.

"Is that little Kitty's voice?" says she. "Is
Kitty in trouble?"

"Mother!" I said once more, and I went forward to meet her, while Mary held back.

"Why—Kitty!" says mother, a slow smile
creeping over her face, and she put both arms
round me. "Kitty!"

Anybody that's known what it is to crave and
thirst for a mother's kiss, when that kiss can't be
had, may guess how I felt to have mother's arms
round me, hugging me in the old fashion, like as
when I was a little child. She laid her cheek on
mine, and made a little crooning sound, as if I was
a baby again, and she petting me.

"Kitty! Little Kitty!" says she. "Come back
to mother at last!"

"O mother, I don't want ever to leave you
again," I sobbed.

"Poor little Kitty!" says she, and she crooned
over me afresh.

I don't know how long that went on; only after
a while I heard Mary say behind, softly, "Now we
ought to go home."

So tears had to stop, for choosing of footsteps,
and I don't know to this day how we got over the
rough ground back to the road. Mother wouldn't

let go of me for a moment, and Mary guided us both. The moon went behind a cloud soon, but it didn't matter, for by that time we had gas-lamps.

All through the longish way back mother clung to me fast, like one who has found a lost treasure. I was that tired at last, I scarce knew how to drag one foot after the other; only I could not complain, I was so happy. And now and then Mary whispered, "Cheer up, Kitty; we'll soon be there! And it's been worth while," says she. And oh, hadn't it been?

Mother didn't talk nor ask any questions. She kept on, in a sort of murmur to herself—"Kitty! little Kitty! my Kitty!"—and that was all.

When we got indoors, Mary lighted a second candle, to brighten up the room. Mother stood holding me fast still, not willing to let go.

"Hadn't Kitty better sit down, Mrs. Phrynne?" says Mary. "She's been on her feet such a time."

"Kitty! yes," mother said. "Kitty's tired! Poor little Kitty!"

"Poor little Kitty!" Mary echoed in a quiet voice. "Did you go to look for Kitty among the rocks, I wonder?"

Mother shook her head. She wouldn't say what took her there, and she never would say nor talk about it afterward. Only, from the day I came back, she stopped all her lonesome walks, and only wanted to have me with her.

I couldn't sit down, mother held me so tight,

and a feeling came as if I should drop if I went on any longer. I'd done a lot that day, you see.

Mary saw, for she always saw everything, and I suppose I did look white. She took a candle, and held it up near my face. Then mother saw too.

"Poor little Kittenkins!" says she tenderly, exactly as father used to do. It had been father's name for me, not mother's.

She put me down on the sofa, just as if I was a little child, and I let her do it. Then she spread a shawl over my feet, and took a chair close by, laying one hand on mine, and sitting there to keep watch.

"Shut your eyes and go to sleep," says she.

Wasn't it sweet to have mother telling me what to do again? I followed her bidding, and sleep wasn't long coming.

When I opened my eyes, mother sat there still. She hadn't stirred a finger. And I had slept two good hours at one stretch.

Mary didn't share mother's room with her that night after all, for mother would have nobody but me; and Mary was only glad to have it so.

CHAPTER XIV.

RUPERT'S RETURN.

No; mother wasn't her old self altogether; I soon found that. The great blow of father's death had left a weakness. She was busy and contented, and didn't murmur; but there was just a touch of weakness. Most likely there always would be, the doctors said.

She took to calling me "Kittenkins" after I came back, and we couldn't cure her of it; so soon we left off trying. It didn't matter, so long as she was pleased.

There was always a sort of petting manner too, as if I was a little child again; and I didn't wish to cure that. Sometimes we fancied she was remembering how bitter she'd been against me, and was trying to make up for it. Any way, I felt I had deserved the bitterness, and I didn't deserve all this love.

Mother would often speak of father, but never of the way he was killed, nor of my wrong behaviour before. Often she called me "Poor little Kittenkins!" in such a grieved voice, I thought she was pitying me for having put him to pain; but one could not be sure.

We soon settled to live in Redland. The surroundings of Claxton would be bad for mother, everybody said, bringing back her great trouble. Besides, Mary could get any amount of work near Bristol, and in Claxton it would be hard to keep ourselves afloat. Mother had a small annuity, but not enough to live on in any comfort.

So I took to dressmaking with Mary, and grew to like it. Redland air suited me, and I got stronger, and was able to sit many hours a day at my needle without suffering. Mother was a help too, only we couldn't let her do very much.

For some months Mary heard almost nothing of Walter or his wife. Then he began to write again, and we soon found out why. He wanted money.

I think our being with Mary was a great protection for her. He couldn't be always running in to screw money out of her, for he didn't care to meet me; and he wouldn't have seen mother on any account, or so we thought.

Mary made it a rule to tell us when she heard from him, and consulted mother what to do when he wanted more money. She said mother was so wonderful clear and sensible on all points of right and wrong, and whether one ought or oughtn't to do a thing. There was a weakness, it is true; but the weakness didn't touch that. And it was hard for Mary to judge, being pulled by her love for

Walter, and yet knowing that the more she helped him the more reckless he grew.

I suppose the "few hundreds" that came with his wife were soon run through. Then he got some sort of situation, and lost it, nobody knew how; but Mary had a pretty clear inkling that it was the old trouble: he couldn't be trusted. And he got another and much poorer situation, and lost that too.

So then he said he would be off to Canada, which was a good thing for Mary and us, but for nobody else. A man that can't succeed in England, because of his unsteadiness and want of right principle, isn't like to do better beyond seas. Why should he? Crossing the ocean don't put right principle nor dependableness into a man!

However, it was settled he should go with his wife and baby—poor little one, to have only such a father to depend on! I couldn't help thinking how different my case had been!

Mary was to give a good big sum out of her hard-won earnings to help them out. Walter wrote lots of letters, full of promises; and Mary sighed over the promises, knowing how little they were worth. What could one expect from a man who would say anything that was convenient at any time, and never trouble himself to keep his word?

We didn't suppose he would come to see Mary before he went, but he did. She had given him so much money, she couldn't afford to go to him; and indeed mother and I hoped they would not meet, for there could be only pain for Mary in seeing him.

Mother could bear to hear Walter's name by this time, near upon three years having gone since father's death; but still she never talked of him without a sort of shudder. I suppose that was the reason why, when Mary heard from Walter that he meant to look in on a certain day, she didn't tell mother nor me a word about it. She only settled for us to go out for a walk. I couldn't think why she was so bent on that, making me leave the sleeve I'd nearly finished, and refusing any delay.

As it happened, never knowing or suspecting that Walter was to be in Redland that day, mother and I for once went towards Bristol, instead of on the Downs. Most likely Mary hadn't a doubt that we should choose the Downs. We didn't, though, for it was close upon Mary's birthday, and mother wanted to choose a present.

So we walked down Park Street, and into Collège Green, and spent a good while looking into the shop windows. Mother had a difficulty in making up her mind what to get, which wasn't like to herself in old days; and I had to help her, and yet seem to leave her free.

At last it was all settled, and we were coming slowly back along the White Ladies Road, having reached a quiet part not far from home, when all at once I saw Walter Russell bearing down upon us at full speed, like a steam-engine.

I don't know how it was we hadn't met him going down. He must have gone round some other way.

Well—there he was; and I saw in a moment that he was changed. His dress was shabby, and his hair wasn't sleek, and he had a sort of uncomfortable down-look, as if he didn't care to meet people. I'm sure he didn't care to meet us, any way. And the jaunty air was gone.

But, besides the change in him, there was a change in me. The three years between seventeen and twenty do make a lot of difference, you know, in a girl's mind and in what she likes. When I saw him there came a sort of wonder—how could I ever have fancied I cared for that man? Had I been crazy?

I didn't think for a moment that mother would notice him. I thought she would pass him by. And I knew he would be glad to rush past, as if he didn't know us. But she gave him a look, and stopped short just in his path. So he couldn't choose but stop too.

"Is that Walter Russell?" says mother, and she turned pale as death, while he went as red as fire.

"Er—yes," says he, with a sort of stammer, as if he wasn't sure.

"Have you been to see Mary?" says mother, fixing her eyes on him, and I saw him shrink under them.

"Yes," says he sheepishly; "just to say good-bye."

I couldn't go on, for mother had hold of my arm, as she always liked to do, and I didn't like to leave her, she looking so white. Mother seemed to forget about me, and Walter and I didn't so much as give a glance one at another.

"Ah!—to say good-bye!" says mother.

"I didn't think it right to go without," mutters he.

"Maybe not," says she; "if it wasn't a solid good-bye in the shape of gold and silver you came to her for, Mr. Russell," says she; and he got as red as fire again. "Ah, I thought so," says she, as quiet as possible. "Mary is a good unselfish creature; but she's got herself to provide for, and there's limits even to what a sister can bear. If I was you, I'd be ashamed to come down on her for help. She, a delicate woman, and you a strong man, with hands of your own, and a head too."

Walter mumbled something about "last time he should be compelled——"

"Well, I hope it is," says she. "There's no sort of being compelled, though, without it is by your own nature. Being compelled to evil means giving in to evil, neither more nor less. And I can tell you, Mr. Russell, I'll do my best to protect Mary and her earnings from you. I say it, and I mean it," says she.

"Much obliged, I'm sure," says he, so I suppose he was angered. "I've got to be off to my train," he says.

"There's no reason why I should keep you,"

says mother. "I'm glad to have seen you this once, and I'm glad to shake hands with you—once —because you have wronged me and mine in the past, and I have much to forgive," says she.

Walter just let her take his hand, and then rushed off as hard as ever he could go. And that was the last I saw of him for many and many a long year—till I was a middle-aged woman, and he was a middle-aged man. He'd lived through a peck of troubles of his own making by then, and he was old before his time, and a poor weak fellow still; but I won't say we hadn't hopes of him. Maybe he'd got some wisdom out of his troubles at last.

Well, to go back to the time I'm telling about.

"Mother, why did you stop him?" I asked.

"I don't know, Kittenkins," says she. " I had a sort of feeling that I must."

"To think that I ever cared for him!" I said.

"I doubt you didn't," says she.

"Oh, but I did, mother."

"You cared a deal for the fuss he made with you," says she. "That's at the bottom of half the silly marriages that's made; and that's a wonderful different thing from caring for himself." And then she says, "He's a bad man."

"He isn't a good man, I'm afraid," said I.

"He's a long way off from that," said she. "There's different sorts of badness, Kitty. A man may be resolute set on evil, or he may drift into evil just from not caring. I don't know as it makes much odds how he comes there—only I'd have more hopes of the resolute man of the two. For if he came out of evil, he'd do it with a will, and stay out; but if Mr. Russell's pulled out, he's as like as not to drift in again."

And wasn't it true?

"Only you wouldn't say there was no hope for a weak man, mother?"

"No," she answered. "There's hope always for every man. God's grace can keep firm the very weakest. All the same," says she, "I'd sooner have to do with a man that's staunch by nature, than with a poor limp thing that's bent by every puff of wind. There's a deal more to be made of the one than the other," says she.

"Rupert wasn't limp," I said; and it was strange I should have spoken of him just then. I don't know why I did, except that he'd been a deal in my thoughts for a great while past. I often wished I could just tell him I was sorry for all the hard words I'd said.

"Rupert? No," says mother. "Rupert was another guess sort of a man. Stuff enough there, Kittenkins. And you might have had him," says she, with a queer look at me; "only you thought you'd sooner have a limp thing for a husband."

"O mother, it's no good to talk of that now," I said. "Rupert's married long ago, I don't doubt."

"I do," says mother, very low.

"And if Mr. Russell wasn't Mary's brother, I'd never give a thought to him again," I said.

"No, and we won't," says mother, and she patted my hand that lay on her arm. She had grown so endearing in her ways, much more than she was used to be before our troubles.

Well, we got home, and mother went upstairs. Mary was in, and I told her all about what had happened.

Mary said, "Ah! I wanted to spare your mother seeing him!"

But I don't think she was sorry it had happened. She put down her work and went after mother.

So I was left alone; and I pulled off my hat and sat down to the sewing-machine. I hadn't been working it for five minutes, when there was a heavy step in the passage—the front door having been left open—and then a tap at the dining-room door.

"Come in," I said.

But there was only a second tap.

"Come in," I said again; and as nobody came in, I got up and opened.

"Does Mrs. Phrynne live here?" says a voice which I seemed to know, yet I didn't directly think whose it was.

A man was standing there, in a big rough great-coat; not very tall, but broad and strong. Our passage was always so dark, I only had a glimpse of a rugged plain sort of face.

"Yes," I said; "this is Mrs. Phrynne's room."

"May I come in?" says he.

"Yes. She is upstairs; but I'll call her," I said.

"No, don't," says he.

R

And he walked in and shut the door. For one second I was frightened ; then—

"Kitty!" says he, "don't you know who I am?"

"Rupert!" I cried out. "O Rupert, I'm so glad!"

The change that came into his face! I don't think words can tell it. I called him "plain" just now, but he wasn't plain then. The ruggedest face can be made beautiful, if the light of a great joy is shining through it.

"Kitty, do you mean it? Kitty, you're not glad really! Tell me that again," says he, all hoarse and shaky.

"Of course I'm glad," said I. "Don't you know how unkind I was before you went away? I have always wanted to tell you I was sorry."

"O Kitty!" says he, and he couldn't go on.

"But you don't know why we are here, or about poor father?" I said.

"Yes, yes, I've heard all," said he. "I went to my mother first, and she and Mr. Armstrong told me everything. But I wouldn't let them write. I wanted to find you out, and see for myself."

He didn't say what it was he wanted to see.

"Where have you been all this while?" I asked. "Sit down, Rupert."

I was noticing how he'd grown taller, and how he was readier in speech, and didn't slouch as he used.

"Ah! I've lots to tell you," said he. "Been in Scotland all this while. Got into a goods-yard, and had to begin at the bottom, as there wasn't anybody to speak for me. And I'm working my way up. But I'll find something to do nearer home, as soon as ever I can. And, Kitty——"

"And you never wrote once to your mother all this while!"

"No," said he, "I didn't; and it's been wrong. I didn't see that so clearly till lately, but it's been wrong, and I told my mother so. She don't mind now, though, now I'm back. And, Kitty——"

I suppose I knew what was coming. Any way, I didn't try to stop it. I just sat still.

And when he asked over again the same question he had asked once before, I never thought of running away. For I was willing to have him.

. . . . . .

We could not marry for a good while. Rupert had to work his way, and he had to look after his mother and sister. He had done wrongly, as he said, staying so long away, and he owed them a lot of help and kindness.

But I promised I would be his wife one day, when the right time should come, which wasn't for a matter of four years and more.

Mother and Mary and Mrs. Bowman and everybody was pleased. Rupert had his faults, there's no doubt; still he had right principle, and he was warm-hearted, and he did work hard and try to get on. Father and mother always had said there was "stuff" in him, and it showed more and more as years went by. Any way, I've never had reason to be sorry for the answer I gave, the second time he asked me to marry him. He's been a good husband to me.

I don't say he has ever been my father's equal, for that he isn't; and Rupert would say so himself. I know he would. But that's not saying he isn't what he is; and I wish there were a lot more men as good as my Rupert.

Twenty years later still, Rupert was appointed stationmaster at Claxton. So then I went back with him to the dear old home of my girlish days.

That's where I have written all this long story.

THE END.

Lightning Source UK Ltd.
Milton Keynes UK
UKOW051014300613

212996UK00001B/44/P